FOR MANY YEARS ROBERT FEARNLEY was the secretary of the UK branch of Pen in Exile, a part of International PEN, which was a centre for exiled writers. He has translated several books of both prose and poetry into English, one of which is *Latvian Tales of Magic*, a collection of old folk stories, which was illustrated by Maija Tabaka, an award-winning Latvian artist.

*Swan Flowers* is his first original work of fiction and combines his two interests of fantasy and medieval England.

I0524566

# SWAN FLOWERS

ROBERT FEARNLEY

SilverWood

Published in 2025 by SilverWood Books

SilverWood Books Ltd
14 Small Street, Bristol, BS1 1DE, United Kingdom
www.silverwoodbooks.co.uk

ISBN 978-1-80042-293-3 (paperback)
Also available as an ebook

British Library Cataloguing in Publication Data
A CIP catalogue record for this book is
available from the British Library

Page design and typesetting by SilverWood Books

# SWAN FLOWERS

# 1

It was a morning when July was in its pride. The temperature was still rising, but Sir Carlyon de Bernedeslaw felt it to be pleasantly comfortable for the day's actions. And yet, he knew that if things were to go awry, he could be dead within the next thirty minutes. Accidents did happen at tourneys, even when friends were jousting. Well, thought Carlyon, I'll not dwell on that. So he told himself, but he knew that defeat at the hands of his boyhood friend, Sir John le Cerre-nore, would mean the death of his hopes, his dreams. Carlyon glanced at his squire, James Morton, who had just helped him on with his helmet and saw that he was being looked at critically.

"Think you something amiss, James?" all, sire, but Sir John is already in the lists. Not good, I ween, to keep him waiting."

"He's ever impatient. Good to make him chafe. I've known him long enow. When impatient, he's wont to act hastily and make mistakes."

At only fifteen years old, James was already as broad across the chest as Carlyon, though not yet so tall, but now he tightened his lips and made no further comment.

Carlyon smiled to himself. Then, taking a breath deep enough to fill his lungs, he adjusted his helmet, so that it rested more comfortably on his hood. Carefully, he checked with his fingers that it fitted. Finally he smoothed down the front of his surtout over his breastplate. He wanted to be sure that his device of a white swan's quill was plainly visible. Taking the gauntlets which James had been holding, he began to draw them on. He knew he needed to concentrate; to channel all his knowledge and skill into what lay ahead of him. At the age of twenty-one he had taken part in many a tournament. This time, however, the stakes were higher.

"Well, James, this next turn of the hourglass is going to change my life, I ween."

"God willing, sire, it'll be for the better. My lady Patrina will be proud of her knight." James cleared his throat, then said, "The time is now, sire. Shall you mount?"

Carlyon looked out briefly through the opening of the pavilion while he steadied his nerves. Then he indicated to James. Resting one hand on his squire's shoulder for support, he stepped up onto the mounting box and, while James moved to hold Champion's head, carefully pulled himself into the saddle. Champion, who had been stamping nervously at the tension, flinched at the sudden weight, but he was calmed by James's experienced hands. Quickly now, James handed up the lance to Carlyon and again held Champion's head. Carlyon put the haft of the lance into its holder on his saddle, and with his left hand he knocked down his visor. There could be no more delay. He felt as though his future happiness – his fate, even – was about to be decided.

"Let's go," he said curtly, his voice a little hoarser than usual.

James chucked at Champion and, when the horse began to move, led him out into the field. As they came round the awning and turned, Carlyon saw Sir John le Cerre-nore, clad forebodingly all in black, already waiting for him at the far end of the list. Carlyon passed out of the shadow into full view, and the late morning sun glinted brightly off the silvery white of his armour. Seeing this, the crowd erupted into an anticipatory roar. Champion's head came up and he would have sidestepped, had James not been holding him firmly. Carlyon lifted a hand to acknowledge the crowd's delight, but he knew that the welcome was not for him personally. It was because they wanted the excitement to begin.

The noise continued while he moved briskly across the field. He could hear horns being blown, as if calling him and John to battle. Above the general clamour he could pick out individual shouts, although their meaning slipped by his consciousness. He could hear dogs barking, and suddenly the neighing of a horse somewhere. Slowly he turned his head slightly to his right in order to take in the colourful scene, restricted as his vision was by his visor grille. There were gaudy pavilions, fluttering flags, the bright dresses of ladies, the drab clothes of country folk. Hawkers were circulating, selling sweetmeats, savouries and fancy goods. People had gathered at Whitewater from all over the land, even from Europe, in order to be present at the royal tournament.

It was a pleasant location. To the east the land undulated gently towards the Trent Valley, and westwards, were Carlyon to lift his eyes, the countryside rose into the distant hills. The field was one of five in England which had been licensed by the Lionheart to host tournaments, and it was a favourite location of Carlyon's. He had jousted there before, but never for so serious a purpose. It was now only a few seconds since he had left the dressing pavilion, but already the rippling atmosphere had smoothed down his nerves and he was ready for the joust. As he rode, he cast his gaze over the palisade to his right. He knew that amongst the crowd there were the Dennetons. There was no time to pick them out, although he expected that they would be sitting close to the royal party. The whole court had come from London with the King, together with many of the country's nobles, all to be there at this grand occasion.

James led Champion across the field. Approaching the end of the tilt, he slowed, then brought the horse to a halt. Carlyon looked down the tilt to where his opponent was waiting. The horse was stamping restlessly, and even at that distance Carlyon could see that John was fidgeting impatiently in the saddle. Carlyon glanced then at the cloth stretched over the tilt – all that would be separating the two jousters. It was fluttering in the breeze, and he hoped it would not make Champion shy. But there was no time to dwell on that. He lowered his lance and prepared himself. James, at Champion's head, had a final few words of advice, and Carlyon had to strain to catch them over the noise of the crowd.

"Remember that Sir John is wont to aim high. He crouches down in his saddle, so his lance tilts up."

Carlyon nodded and nervously adjusted the position of his own lance, as if in response. The crowd was calling out support for both men, but Carlyon had no mind to distinguish individual shouts. He focused his mind on his opponent. The sun, high in the sky, was behind him and slightly off to his left side. This meant that for the first sally he would have whatever advantage there was. Should there be a second, then any advantage would fall to John. These thoughts were only momentary, almost unformed, in the few seconds of expectation. Then James was moving sideways while still keeping a calming hand on Champion's head. He had been watching. When the signal was given, he slapped the brightly coloured cloth that was stretched over Champion's flank.

The horse broke into a canter, and then a steady lope. Carlyon met John short of the midway point. John had moved faster, keen to seek an advantage. The tactic seemed to work. His lance was direct to target. Even so, Carlyon saw it coming and twisted his body. The coronall of John's lance ripped his surtout, but slid across his breastplate; harmless except for taking his breath. Carlyon's lance caught John, but because of Carlyon's contortions there was no force behind it. John barely flinched. Relieved at still being in the saddle, Carlyon checked Champion with the reins. The horse slowed his gait and blew out through his nostrils; as much, it seemed, through excitement as through exertion. Carlyon turned the horse and rubbed his neck slightly to calm him. Then they walked slowly to the start for the second joust.

James came running up to the new end and again held Champion's head. He looked up at Carlyon and offered words of encouragement. "You avoided that one, sire. You have his measure now."

Carlyon was not so sure of that, but he smiled beneath his helmet. There was a slight delay while the coronall on John's lance was checked. Then the signal was given.

The tension seemed to slip away from Carlyon as he picked up speed. This time they were closer to the midpoint when he and John met. Again John's aim was true. Carlyon would have been unseated had it caught him more squarely. He slipped sideways to the right, but fortunately his left foot stayed in the stirrup. Miraculously almost, he kept himself in the saddle, although he was unable to explain how. Even so, in his efforts to remain upright he lost his grip on his lance and it clattered to the ground. Clumsily, he pulled at the reins. Then as Champion slowed, he recovered his position and tried to regain some composure. Dismay was dimming the sun for him. He had scored no hit at all that time. He seemed to have no answer to John's skill. The crowd was shouting, but Carlyon didn't look. There was a particular lady in the crowd, but he was sure that she would not have been impressed by his display. Perhaps, even, she was no longer concentrating on him? His dream was close to being dispersed, as if, despite the summer sunshine, he had awoken to a cold and frosty morning. There was only one more sally and his future hopes were suddenly unsure.

Carlyon sat on his horse at the end of the tilt, the sun glittering off the silvery-white steel plate protecting his limbs. Champion was standing calmly. Carlyon himself seemed impassive, hidden by his helmet, but his left hand gripping the reins and his right hand gripping the pommel were both tightly tensed. James was beside him. His face was screwed up in concentration as he and a steward carefully examined the lance, which he had picked up from where Carlyon had let it fall. Satisfied that it was undamaged, James handed it up to the waiting knight. Carlyon laid it across his saddle in the attack position and tested his grip on the haft. Blowing out his breath in what was almost a sigh, he signalled to the marshal that he was ready. There was no point in waiting. The sooner it was over, the better.

"Could you lower the point of your lance, sire?" James called to him urgently. "It's aiming too high. Twist your body as you approach Sir John, and aim lower."

Carlyon nodded and adjusted the position of his lance. Nervously, he moved his feet to pull his stirrups back slightly and leaned forward, ready for the signal. When it came, he concentrated grimly on the approaching figure of his opponent, as Champion picked up speed. Clad entirely in a blackness relieved only by the golden device of a lion's head, John was bearing down on him like an avenging spectre. Despite the tension, Carlyon was strangely able to see how John was crouching in the saddle, as if trying to get behind his horse's neck. Carlyon raised himself slightly in his stirrups to try to lessen the bouncing effect of Champion's pounding hooves. Ready for the thrust, he gripped his lance more tightly.

In the few seconds of the joust, he clearly sensed John's confidence. Then his opponent was upon him. Twisting his body, but leaning forward slightly, Carlyon thrust out with all the strength his arm could find. It was as if he knew that it was all or nothing. It was a final throw, but this time it was direct on target. John's tactic during this third sally was the same as the first two which had almost given him success, except that he too twisted his body slightly. As a result, Carlyon's lance caught him squarely, a flashing instant before John was ready to hit Carlyon. That was of no consequence, however. Seemingly assured of his victory and thinking of hitting his opponent, John had momentarily loosened his grip on the reins. Sensing the slight slackening of control, his horse tossed its head to the right, as if wanting to veer away from the approaching horse and rider on the other side of the tilt. John's rhythm was interrupted. Carlyon's hit happened to catch him in just such a way, while he was distracted, that the force pushed him sideways. The arrogant looseness of John's feet in the stirrups was unable to keep him in the saddle. As his horse faltered momentarily, he fell to the ground. Carlyon galloped on, surprised that he had not been hit, but even more surprised at the sounds behind him, which told him of his success. He pulled at the reins to check Champion and glanced back. John was on the ground, and as Carlyon turned his head back to the front, exhilaration shivered through him like a cooling breeze. Slowly, Champion came to a stop and Carlyon rested his lance on his left arm, so that his right hand could pat his horse's neck. Champion's calm strength had helped him to win the day. Carlyon turned again to look at John, who had by now been helped to his feet by his squire. John took off a gauntlet and waved to Carlyon, to show that he was not seriously hurt.

Carlyon acknowledged him with an upward tip of his lance, and clicked Champion into motion. As he gripped the reins to pull the horse round, he noticed that he was trembling. The noise from the crowd had become a buzzing in his ears, as indistinguishable thoughts swarmed through his brain. He breathed in deeply and felt his head begin to clear. The crowd, which had been a homogeneous mass, now began to separate into individuals as he rode nearer, and he picked out his objective: the King and the royal party. Pulling Champion to a halt at a respectful distance, Carlyon took off his helmet and handed it to James, who had come running across to meet him. Carlyon shook his head slightly in its freedom, put his lance into its rest position, and then bowed to the King, who smiled pleasantly at him.

"Well done, Sir Carlyon. An excellent joust. Although I fancy fortune smiled on you."

"You fought well, Sir Knight," added the Queen graciously. "I thought me Sir John would have the better of you."

"I thank Your Majesties for your praise. I had a worthy opponent and he was unlucky today."

The King nodded at Carlyon's show of modesty, and the Queen held out a small kerchief.

"Take this favour and give it to your lady," she told him.

Carlyon held up his lance and the Queen fastened the kerchief on the end. He bowed in gratitude, turned Champion, and rode off down the palisade. It was but a few yards, and he stopped in front of where a young woman was sitting with her father. She was looking expectantly at Carlyon, who had made a promise to her before the tournament. He took off his right gauntlet and patted Champion's neck to calm him. Then he looked up at the lady Patrina. Her slim body, in its deep blue woollen gown and pale yellow supertunic, was leaning forward slightly, almost as if she could reach out to him. But Carlyon was looking at her face. Her braided hair was held off her face, and so he could look directly into her alluring hazel eyes. He smiled at her, and then he looked at her father.

"By your leave, my lord?" he asked.

The Earl of Denneton, an elderly man whose body still bore the build of his fighting youth, nodded approvingly and his rheumy brown eyes widened in pleasure.

Carlyon lifted up his lance towards the earl's excited daughter. "I promised I would dedicate my victory to you, my lady. Here is a favour for you."

Patrina's eyes danced with delight as she took the kerchief and pleasure made her hunch up her shoulders. Carlyon's lips parted in his happiness. When he had made the promise, he had not really expected to be able to keep it. Patrina put the kerchief to her lips, and Carlyon smiled at her romantic gesture. Her bright eyes seemed to be calling to his heart, and when she lifted her head momentarily, his breath caught in his mouth at the beauty of her long white neck.

"Thank you, sir," she said, somewhat formally, but with no trace of shyness.

Carlyon inclined his head in acceptance and, with a nod also of acknowledgement to her father, who was smiling indulgently, he wheeled Champion round and rode off to the dressing tent. When he got there, clumping in a little shyly through the congratulations which he received, he found that John had already almost finished changing. Before he could ask him if he was injured, Carlyon was greeted heartily.

"All praise to the victor! And was Her Majesty pleased with your performance?"

"Indeed she was." Carlyon was surprised that he could detect no rancour in John's voice, because he knew that he had been lucky. He masked his embarrassment by holding out his arms so that James could begin to take off his armour. He spoke again without looking at John. "She told me she thought you would be the victor."

"Hah! She did, did she? I think so. You were lucky. I should have won."

Carlyon glanced at him, sensing unhappiness, but John went on.

"It was God's will and we must accept it. There'll be another time and I'll try to win. I'll make sure I win." His voice suddenly changed as he shouted at his squire. "Give me that, you knave! You're as slow as a pregnant ass!" He cuffed the unfortunate youth, who quickly handed over the belted dagger, but almost immediately John recovered his good spirits. He broke wind, which seemed to ease him, and continued his interrupted conversation with the other knights.

Carlyon took his time over changing, and when he was satisfied with his appearance, he moved towards the pavilion's opening. The afternoon's jousting was about to begin and he was anxious for better company than John's, so he went swiftly round the field to where Lady Patrina and her father were sitting and climbed up onto the benches. The earl saw him and brightly indicated to him to come and join them. Father and daughter made room for him to sit, and Carlyon hid his disappointment with a smile, for the earl had indicated a place next to him, which put him between Carlyon and his daughter.

The earl gave him no time to dwell on that. "Rest yourself there, young fellow. 'Sblood, it was a brave fight! What a pity your father wasn't here to see it. He'll be so proud when you tell him. He and I had many a joust when we were younger."

Although now carrying extra weight on his abdomen and with a face that had become fleshy, the earl was still a fine figure of a man, and he wandered off into a tale about a success of his in his younger days. Carlyon listened politely, encouraged by noticing that Patrina was smiling fondly at him.

When the earl paused, Carlyon said, "I wish I could have seen you fight, my lord. My father's told me of your skill."

The earl nodded, accepting the flattery without thought. He lifted his cap and lightly scratched the bald strip down the middle of his head, which was glistening with sweat. "You've some skill yourself," he said. "Your father's spoken to me about his hopes for you. You need more practice. Sir John fought well. He's a skilful jouster. You were lucky to beat him, but I'm pleased for you. Now, what you must do is strengthen your arm, so that you can hold the lance more firmly and thrust more strongly. You need to find better exercises than holding a quill pen."

He laughed heartily at his little quip. Carlyon thought it good to join him, even though he was not amused by the old man's slightly contemptuous dig at his liking for writing poetry. He was keen to speak to Patrina, and wishing that he was sat next to her.

Then the earl unexpectedly slapped his thigh. "'Sblood!" he said. "Did you see that sally? Here, change places with me and you two young folk can have a chat. I want to concentrate on this bout."

The change was quickly made and Carlyon turned to the eagerly awaiting Patrina. He saw that she had placed the kerchief which he had given her in the top of her bodice so that she could touch it from time to time. His gaze moved up over the smooth white skin of her long neck, past the slightly moist lips of her pert mouth, and stopped at her sparkling hazel eyes.

"Have you enjoyed today's jousts, my lady?" he asked as an opener.

"Oh yes! It's been so exciting. It looked so dangerous. I almost thought me I'd swoon for very fear. Especially for one in particular."

She smiled archly at him, and both knew without explanation which one she meant. He nodded, but was too modest to follow that line. Instead...

"There are many ladies here from the court, aren't there? Have you had an audience with the Queen yet?"

Given a cue, Patrina spoke enthusiastically about the Queen, her ladies and their fashions. From that, their conversation moved on to other topics and the afternoon passed enjoyably.

The setting sun was laying out long tongues of shadow across the field by the time the day's sport was over and Carlyon and Patrina had to part. Carlyon was staying at Tickhill during the tourney. This was some miles away from the Dennetons' lodgings, but it was understood that he would join them the next day.

John was also staying at Tickhill, and when they had eaten their supper that evening, the two of them stayed in the castle's great hall to drink and chat. A lazy atmosphere surrounded them, as if, although July, a fire had been laid and its smoke was swirling above their heads. After the sun had set, they continued to sit in the gloom, while rushes were lit on the walls.

Then, almost as Carlyon was about to suggest retiring for the night, John remarked idly, "I noticed you spent the afternoon with my lord Denneton and his daughter. I knew not you were so close acquainted?"

"The earl's an old acquaintance of my father's. The family's originally from Lancashire, but the late earl brought the family south to be near the court. They have property hard by Chertsey."

"And his daughter? Is she promised to anyone?"

"Lady Patrina? No, she's not promised yet. Perhaps before long."

"I wouldn't call her a beauty. What would she have to offer?"

"I find her beautiful. She has a simple, quiet beauty that grows on acquaintance. And she has a very lovely nature."

"Mayhap so. I think she'll need it. But will she come with a good dowry?"

"It's expected. She's the only daughter, so she'll be well provided for."

"Indeed. Had I won today, I would have dedicated my victory to Lord Acklam's daughter. You know, the tall blonde one with the beautiful neck. They say she'll get a good dowry: two estates in Yorkshire." John fell silent, as if thinking. He finished off his wine and seemed about to leave his seat, but before he did, he spoke again. "You know much about this lady. Do you have intentions?"

Carlyon moved slightly from side to side. Nervously, he squeezed his nostrils between his thumb and forefinger and then rubbed the finger over the tip of his nose. He would not have spoken on such a personal matter, but alcohol had loosened the ties of his inhibitions. "I'm very attracted to her. I'd like to marry her. I think my father would be happy."

"If he would, then her dowry would be satisfactory." John narrowed his eyes in the flickering light and looked at Carlyon. "I'm looking for a satisfactory dowry myself. I suppose Lady Patrina is comely enough to attract suitors. I'd have to look at her more closely."

"Do that, and your eyes will find my blade in their way. Lady Patrina is not the one for you. Stay away!"

"Ha, ha! I'd expect more beauty. But she'll be beautiful enough for you. Are you going to make a declaration?"

Carlyon looked morosely at his goblet. The wine was not really helping him. "I must speak to her father. I know he likes me, but he may be after a better match for his only daughter. I think me also that Lady Patrina has romantic dreams about dashing knights."

John laughed again, but in a kindly way, and said, "Don't be shy, Sir Poet. Write her some of your love verses and you'll win her heart. Don't let your heart be faint for this fair lady."

Carlyon shook his head, but it was more in acceptance than in refusal, and both men rose from their seats to retire for the night.

In his bed, Carlyon lay awake for some time, as his mind rattled loudly with thoughts of Patrina. Then, worriedly, he thought of John. Had he taken an interest in her? Was he lying in his bed and considering her possible attractions? Carlyon shifted awkwardly under his blanket, as he tried to move away from such prickling thoughts. Restful sleep was some while in coming.

Carlyon continued to spend time with the Dennetons over the following two days. John gave him no further grounds for worry until the close of the tournament. On the afternoon of the final day, when everyone was preparing to leave Whitewater, John sought out Carlyon to ask about travelling home.

"The court will be spending the night at Clipstone. They leave for Newark first thing tomorrow and they'll travel back to London through Stamford. Shall we go with them?"

"No, I'm travelling back with the Dennetons. They're going through Leicester to visit relations and Lady Patrina suggested I travel with them. I think she likes me." Carlyon had got the impression that Patrina's suggestion had been almost an idle one on the spur of the moment, but he had seized on it.

John was characteristically dismissive. "She probably wants to show off a knight to her cousins. That's all it is. Aah! Perhaps I should join you. I'll show you how to win a lady."

Carlyon looked sharply at his friend. He knew that John was speaking seriously and that he thought nothing of playing with a lady's heart. Anxiety at this new situation brought saliva into his mouth. "You're not interested in Lady Patrina, are you?" he asked. "I thought your intentions were towards Lord Acklam's daughter?"

"It makes no difference to me. A pretty face and a good dowry. Well, I could win Lady Patrina's heart if I wished, but not this time. I'm travelling with the court. I want to advance my prospects with the King. Then I'll look at other prospects. I'll call on the Dennetons after Michaelmas and see how you've got on."

Carlyon smiled quietly, relieved that John had been speaking boastfully, as he often did. It seemed that they would not be rivals in this matter. He spent a restful night, and early the following morning he went over to Worksop Manor, where the Dennetons had been staying. They were almost ready to depart. The day had dawned somewhat cooler than during the past week, and although summer was still sprawled across the fields, cloud had slyly drifted into the sky to block the sun from time to time. Carlyon was unconcerned. He was receiving his sunshine from another source, and he expected the day to be fine enough for his purposes.

Carlyon accompanied the Dennetons for part of the way. Then he bade farewell to the earl, because he had to go home to his father. He was unhappy about leaving, because he knew from comments made that the old man was aware of his interest in Patrina. The earl's behaviour led him to believe that if there was no outright encouragement, at least there was no disapproval.

As they parted, the earl told Carlyon to greet his father for him. "I hope to see him at court before Christmas."

"He'll want to see you. I know he bears great love for you, my lord."

"And I for him. 'Sblood! He was always a good friend to me. He must come to Chertsey before too long. And you, young man – you must also be sure to come to visit us soon."

"Thank you, my lord. I look forward to seeing you again." Carlyon smiled at the earl, but he was conscious of Patrina looking at him from the wagon. He turned his body slightly in the saddle and bowed to her. "Fare you well, my lady. God protect you and see you safely home."

"Farewell, Sir Knight. Your company has been a pleasure and I hope to see you at Chertsey."

"Quite so!"

Carlyon's head snapped back as the earl's brusque words rang out, but he saw a smile hiding in the corners of his mouth. He realised that the earl was keeping control. No matter. He would speak to his father about his hopes. Then he would go to Chertsey. Bowing politely to the old man, he clicked Champion into motion and set off for home.

# 2

Summer was long gone on the wings of departing swallows before Carlyon was able to pay a visit to the Dennetons. To his irritation, his father kept him at home to deal with a family matter and it was drawing close to All Souls' Day before he could set off for Chertsey, taking with him two hawks as a gift from his father.

The earl accepted them gratefully and his florid face rippled with pleasure. "I'll give them a try on the morrow. You'll come with me. We have an excellent country hereabouts. You'll enjoy it."

The earl wanted to talk about hunting and Carlyon had to humour him, putting into his voice an enthusiasm that was only lukewarm. Then eventually he was able to ask after Lady Patrina without it seeming too obvious. At least, the earl seemed not to notice any awkwardness.

"She's keeping well. Has a head full of romantic notions. That young fellow, Sir John le Cerre-nore, is encouraging it, I think."

Carlyon's face jerked. His breath stopped, hot in his chest, but the earl's attention was on his new hawks as he rubbed the side of a finger down the neck of one of them.

"Sir John? Is he here?" Carlyon asked, surprise giving his voice an anxiously higher pitch than usual.

"Sir John?" The earl looked up, as if he had received an unexpected question. "Oh, aye, he's been here a week or so. Comes out hunting with me. Very good. He catches more than I do, the young rapscallion." The earl laughed, and Carlyon wondered at his good humour.

As soon as he could, he left and hurried away to seek out John. His worried search ended in the armoury, where John was having a dagger re-hafted. At the sound of Carlyon's entrance, he turned his head. Seeing who it was, delight pulled his mouth into a grin and he swiftly got to his feet.

"Carlyon!" he called. "My heart leaps to see you! My lady Patrina has been wondering if you would come. I'm so glad you're here. We'll have some amusement now."

Carlyon submitted to John's boisterous embrace, but when they disengaged, he got straight to the point. "I didn't expect to see you here."

"Why not? I expected to see you. Has your ardour for my lady cooled?"

"No, it hasn't. I was delayed by family business. I'm hoping to press my suit, now I am here."

"Are you so? Hm, I'd seek to do that myself."

Despite a slight note of apology which he caught in John's voice, Carlyon looked at him angrily. His fist clenched, but he pulled calmness round him like a cloak. "I thought me you had no interest in Patrina. You slighted somewhat her beauty, I trow."

"I wasn't interested, but she will receive an excellent dowry. I fancy she'll make a good wife, in spite of her daydreaming. She'll not need romance after I've won her."

"You sound confident. I'm still in the lists and I fancy I'll prove the better man."

John laughed amiably and put a friendly arm round Carlyon's shoulders. Carlyon stiffened slightly, but John told him that he was looking forward to the contest and that they would have some fun. John's jolly mood grated somewhat with Carlyon. He had known him for so long, and he loved him almost like a brother. They had had many a contest in the past, but this was much more than a game for Carlyon. He knew also that John would take winning seriously. This was not what he had been dreaming of.

When Patrina came out of the ladies' quarters to join everyone for supper later that day, she greeted Carlyon warmly. He was sure that she was glad to see him, but he could not but notice that she seemed equally friendly towards John.

Over the following days Carlyon set out to do what he could to impress both Patrina and her father. He found that John seemed to have the same intention, and the implicit competition between the two of them both spurred him and irritated him.

One morning there was a mock tourney in the yard. To Carlyon's chagrin, he was easily bested, because although he was stockily built, John's beefier frame and extra couple of inches in height gave him an advantage. Nevertheless, Carlyon felt that he put on a good performance. At least Patrina congratulated him.

"Saw you that?" he told John later. "My lady was pleased with my performance."

"Yes – pleased to console the loser," laughed John. "To me, she gave the prize as victor."

"So be it. Yet to win a battle is not to win a war."

One evening each of them produced a love poem which he had written. Carlyon put his heart into his and was sure that the sincere sentiment contrasted sharply with John's pedestrian technical exactitude. That seemed to be the opinion of the audience, but

Carlyon was again chagrined when Patrina congratulated both of them equally warmly. He wondered if she was unable to tell the difference between a good poem and an indifferent one, but then the silver spindles of his brain flashed with a suspicion that she was enjoying the competition. It was as if she wanted to keep it running.

Neither man was able to see Patrina alone, although one evening Carlyon was accosted by a gleeful John with what seemed like disturbing news.

"Ho, Carlyon! What think you of this? I was in my lady Patrina's quarters this afternoon!"

Jealousy burned through Carlyon's limbs as if they were desiccated, but he maintained a calmness and asked, "Pray, how was that?"

"No great difficulty. I borrowed me a cloak and, thus masked, I was able to slip in unchallenged."

"And what did my lady have to say to you, when you found her?"

"Hm. Nothing, I fear. The rooms were empty. It seems that the ladies had all gone out to the chapel for some purpose."

Carlyon set his face grimly. He refused to encourage John by talking more about it, but he knew that he would have to work faster.

Early in the afternoon of the following day, he lurked in a passageway along which he knew that Patrina would have to pass to reach the great hall for dinner. He was rewarded when she and her aunt appeared. When Patrina saw him, he heard her make a remark to her aunt about outlaws lying in wait, but he saw the laughter in her face and knew that she was teasing. He had been unable to think of a clear excuse for his presence there, so he carried on without it.

"Good day, ladies. Are you going in for dinner?"

"We are, young man," said the aunt, looking at him with what seemed to be an amused smile. "Will you be so kind as to escort us?"

Relieved, Carlyon stepped in beside them, but made sure that he was next to Patrina. She smiled at him and asked where Sir John was. Carlyon looked at her sharply and was only slightly mollified to see a twinkle in her eyes. He was in no mood for teasing.

"Would you prefer to see him?" he asked sourly.

"Not only. I like to see the two of you. You and Sir John are old friends, are you not?"

"Indeed so, my lady. We were boys together on neighbouring estates. We've been companions and rivals in many things. But I think me there is a time when enough will suffice."

"Oh, I know nought of that, Sir Carlyon. It's a lucky maiden who has two knights eager to do her bidding. You and Sir John would do anything I asked, wouldn't you?"

"I would, and willingly. You only have to ask."

"Thank you, Sir Knight. If ever I'm in distress, I'll be sure to call on you. But I'm sure Sir John would also be willing to come to my rescue."

"Perhaps he would. But surely you would have a preference?"

Carlyon wondered if he had gone too far by asking that, but he knew that an answer could show him whether he was on a hopeless chase. He glanced sideways at Patrina, and saw her shake her head so that the silk of her headdress rustled.

"I know not that I may," she said with a smile, while looking at him from under her eyelashes. "It would be so difficult to choose between the two of you."

Carlyon tightened his lips in vexation and wondered if she was being serious. Unconsciously, nervousness made him briefly pinch his nostrils between his thumb and forefinger. He struggled to find something else to say, but was saved by their arrival at the entrance to the great hall. He stood aside while the ladies washed their hands in the bowl of water by the door. Then he was gratified that they waited until he had done the same, so that they could continue to the table together. At least he had that small victory for his effort.

A few days later, Carlyon was walking across the yard from the main gate when he was hailed by John. Changing direction slightly, he walked towards him, while John hurried more quickly in his direction, as if time was being lost. John began to speak before he was close, saying that he had been looking for Carlyon.

"I've not been far away," Carlyon told him equably, attempting to ignore the arrogant tone of excitement in John's voice. His own voice was like a restraining hand on the other's mouth. "The brother of one of the ostlers died of a fever a few weeks past. I've been to take some food to his widow and her children."

"You've been taking charity? Are you thinking of becoming a friar?" John was so surprised that he forgot his own business in the face of this news.

"They're very poor and have been suffering greatly. I only did a little."

"Why do you bother with these paupers? You're always doing things like that."

29

"I do what I can to help. And I can see nothing wrong in that."

"You're wasting your time. The more you help, the more there is to do. You should leave charity to the Church. I do. That's where saints belong."

"Of course." Carlyon tossed his head, as if trying to shake away drops of embarrassment. He decided to change the subject. Glancing up at the greying sky, he said, "It's getting late in the afternoon now. Shall we go and find a drink?"

"Good idea. I need a drink. I've got something to celebrate."

John's excitement seemed under control now, because despite Carlyon's interested query as to what he could be celebrating, he grabbed his arm to pull him away, and said that he would tell him over a drink. When they were sitting in a small pantry with their drinks, John put both his elbows on the table and leaned forward to look closely at Carlyon opposite him.

"While you were busying yourself with paupers, I've been with the earl," he announced with a triumphant smirk.

Carlyon tensed his shoulders, but said nothing as John continued.

"I told him that I wish to marry his daughter. What think you of that?"

# 3

*W*hen John told Carlyon that he had asked the earl if he could marry Patrina, Carlyon said nothing, despite John's request for his opinion. He looked straight at John's face, which seemed to be glowing, even in the dim light of the pantry. Grimly, he held his body with restraints of stiff determination. This was nonsense. He was in love with Patrina, whereas he suspected that John was merely interested in her dowry. However, even as the blood was roaring through his ears, he was determined to show no weakness in front of John. He drew in a breath and let it out again slowly, while the pistons of his mind clanked rustily, unable to find any words to express his thoughts.

It was only a few seconds later when John impatiently began to speak again. "His Lordship was impressed. I reminded him I was a champion knight. And I'm a very good hunter. He's seen the trophies I've got while I've been here. More than he has. He knows who my father is, so he knows my family isn't unworthy of his daughter. I told him what property I'll be bringing to the marriage, to join what he'll give. I thought it good to suggest what property should be in the dowry. He's a sensible man. He knows that there'll be negotiations for these things, and the earlier they start, the better." At last he paused and, almost as if unconsciously, broke wind and let out his breath in relief. Then he took a good drink of his wine.

Carlyon also took a drink, and with the lubrication he was able to speak. "When is the wedding to be?" he asked, making no effort to sound pleased.

"No date yet. The earl said he'd think about it. He had some notion about speaking to my lady first. They'd better not be too long. I won't be kept waiting for a woman. He won't find a handsomer or a braver man for his daughter. He should be glad to have me take her off his hands. I expect he'll speak to me soon and we'll agree the final arrangements."

Carlyon looked at him. A slight curl of contempt was pulling at the corner of his mouth. He had noticed that John had said nothing about love. That would surely give him an advantage over John, for he was sure that Lady Patrina desired to be loved. The shock which he had felt at John's unexpected swiftness was subsiding, and when he spoke, his voice was calm and measured. "You boast too soon, John. I'm in love with Lady Patrina. She's the lady of my heart, the dream for whom I'll do anything. I hardly thought me you'd move so quickly."

"That's the way of it, Carlyon. I know how you feel about her, but she'll be a good wife for me. She's pretty enough and she has a good dowry promised, so I can love her also. You were always too slow. You spend too much time thinking, when you should be acting."

"Do I indeed? Well, I'm going to act now." Carlyon finished off his goblet of wine. "I won't let you take this prize. The fight is not yet over. I'm going to speak to the earl and tell him that I also want to marry Lady Patrina. I'm as brave a knight as you are, and

32

I'll have lands enough to bring to the marriage. Were I to marry Lady Patrina, I would worship her as a queen. She would be my breath, my blood, my life. I'll go straight away and seek audience with the earl."

John did not seem surprised or worried by this speech. He nodded and a jolly smile lit up his face. "You go ahead and do that. We'll let the earl choose."

Carlyon looked at him narrowly, but realised that it was John's confidence that was forming his words. He was so sure that the earl would prefer him. Carlyon nodded at his rival and went off to seek admittance to the earl's chamber.

He was received kindly, but even so, nervousness seemed to have cast a sheet of rust over his movements. He had never spoken to a maiden's father about marriage before, and perhaps, had it not been for John, he would not have been doing so now. He would have asked his father to approach Patrina's. That would have been so much easier. When Carlyon announced that he wanted to speak on an important matter, the earl inclined his head in acknowledgement and got himself ready to listen. Carlyon cranked up his spine and began by complimenting the earl on his beautiful daughter, who had so many graces and accomplishments which reflected well on him. Unsure how this was going down, as the earl merely looked at him with a slight smile on his face, Carlyon decided to jump straight in.

"I'll be most honoured if I can be allowed to marry my lady. I'll serve her well and be a credit to you, my lord."

The earl still said nothing, still smiled slightly, but there was nothing in his demeanour that was discouraging, so Carlyon ploughed on.

"I'd be the happiest man in Christendom, and she were my wife. I would love and cherish her always. I'd be her shining knight. I beg, my lord, that you look on my suit with favour."

He paused there, wondering what he could say next without repeating himself, but it seemed that the earl was ready to speak. He smiled broadly in a friendly way that sent a shaft of optimism into Carlyon's breast.

"It surprises me not to hear what you've just told me, Sir Knight. I've been watching you and I've noticed your interest in my daughter. I'm fond of you and I know your family well. I have to tell you, I'd not considered anyone for a marriage with Patsy yet – but perhaps it is time to think of such a thing. She has suddenly become a woman, I see. Your friend, Sir John, has also spoken to me today about marrying her." He paused and looked at Carlyon, who merely nodded as this was not news to him, and so the earl continued. "I'll speak to Patsy and tell her that she has two suitors, but I fancy she may already have guessed. She'll have seen how the two of you have been behaving these past two weeks. I'll write to your father and we'll speak on this matter again."

Later that evening, before Patrina went to bed, she asked her aunt, a twice-widowed woman, for her opinion of her two suitors. She knew that her aunt, as everyone else seemed to have done, had noticed the rivalry between the two knights and the attentions which were being paid to her niece.

"They're both handsome, are they not?" said Patrina. "Sir John is taller and perhaps a little more strongly built, but I think me Sir Carlyon would be a more interesting companion. And he does have the most lovely green eyes."

Her aunt said that she thought that her brother, Patrina's father, would prefer Sir Carlyon, because he was of the better family.

"But would he be the better husband?" asked Patrina. "I'm sure he'll do anything for me, anything to win me."

"Mayhap. He's a dreamer, I ween, but I fancy he'll try. However, my dear, there's more to marriage than dashing deeds and romantic songs."

"Think you so? I think that would be lovely. I want to be worshipped." Patrina paused to help her aunt, who was taking off her barbette to let her hair loose. Patrina took the linen band and ran it through her fingers, dreaming momentarily of the time when she would be able to put up her own hair. The thought of marriage was growing warmer. It was almost as if she sensed fulfilment in that state. She handed the barbette over to her aunt's maid and then held her aunt's hand affectionately. "But do you like Sir John also?"

"He's a very different man, my dear. He'll not be led by a silken girdle. But you need fear no enemies when he's your protector."

Patrina hunched her shoulders and let a murmur of delight slip out through her lips. "He speaks plainly. I'm not sure that I don't like that rough way of speaking. He'll tell me what to do and I could run at his bidding."

"Being seated on a monument, receiving flowers, is safe, my dear. But to live with a lion could be dangerous."

"But how exciting! I'm sure, if Sir John were to love me, that I'll be able to keep him to my whistle. Oh, Aunt! Which one can I choose?"

"It'll be best if you're guided by your father."

"How boring! I must set them a task and then choose."

The following evening the assembled company was entertained by a minstrel. At first Carlyon had not expected much. The man's tunic was dirty and frayed, and occasionally when he moved Carlyon could see a hole below the armpit of the left sleeve. His hose too were dirty, and his belt was a simple hempen cord. Seemingly unabashed at his appearance, however, the man seated himself on a stool near the fireplace and took up a stringed instrument that had seen better days.

From where Carlyon was sitting, he had a clear view of the minstrel in the flickering firelight, and he watched with interest as he tuned up his instrument. He wondered what it would be like to be able to play and sing; to make music for his poems and to sing them rather than recite them. Then an idea came to him: he would speak to the minstrel afterwards and ask him to put one of his poems to music. Then he would pay him to sing it outside Patrina's chamber when she was taking her afternoon rest. Surely she would find that romantic?

While he was reviewing which of his poems would be most suitable, the earl gave a signal and the minstrel began his first ballad. Conversations still continued around the table, but the singer had a strong voice and Carlyon could hear him clearly. To his pleasure, the voice was mellifluous and attractive. Patrina would be certain to enjoy listening to it. Glancing at her, he saw that she was already watching the singer intently, as if trying to draw his words into her enraptured face. Carlyon felt a stab of jealousy flash through him. Looking back towards the fireplace, he dreamed about what it would be like to be a wandering minstrel, able to hold people's attention wherever one sat down to play. Then he smiled, as he accepted that even a lady with Patrina's romantic soul would never see a man behind the voice of a low-born minstrel. He left his idle thoughts and concentrated on the singer's words, while he kept glancing at Patrina, hoping to catch her eye, if she should look his way.

The minstrel sang several ballads, lubricated by swigs of small ale, but it was the final one that seemed to hold Patrina's attention the most. Carlyon, dreaming of her as he watched, missed the start of the song. When his attention did turn to it, attracted by its pleasant melody, he found that it was about a swan which was injured by a hunter. The swan, knowing that it was going to die, flew away to a secret place, which swans always tried to reach, in order to die there. When the dying swan reached this place, it sang its thrilling swansong and then, at peace, it breathed its last. Once it was dead, however, beautiful white flowers sprang up where its body lay, and these flowers of the swan then bloomed for a year and a day.

When the last notes of the song died away, Patrina immediately called out her appreciation, surprising Carlyon with her enthusiasm, as if she had poked him. "What a lovely story! Is it really true? Is that what swans do?"

"I've heard it to be so, my lady," said the minstrel. "They say that such a place exists, and that a man who watches in secret will be able to hear the swan's song and then pick its flowers to carry away to his true love."

"Oh, how romantic! How I would love to have some of those flowers. If only I had a knight who would do that for me."

She clapped her hands together, and Carlyon looked at her excited face. She was like a child reaching for a shiny bauble, and he wished that he had such a bauble that was easily plucked. He would give it to her, driven to make her happy. Then a cackle of harsh laughter interrupted his thoughts and his gaze snapped onto John's amused face.

"That's a silly thing to wish for, my lady. Why those? You can pick whatever flowers you wish, if you like posies and that sort of thing. But knights don't go to collect flowers. There's nothing dangerous or brave in that. Perhaps boys and poets might do it."

A shadow of cold disappointment slipped across Patrina's face, as if each of John's words were a fold of a curtain, and seeing it, Carlyon's heart seemed to bump into his throat with sadness. At that moment a visionary fervour seized him and he would have done anything to make Patrina happy.

"I can understand why you should want those flowers of the swan, my lady," he said quietly, but distinctly. "They must be beautiful – just as you are beautiful."

"I knew that you'd understand, Sir Carlyon. Oh, I would so like some of those flowers."

She sighed and looked at him imploringly. Her eyes caught the flame of a nearby light and glinted enticingly. Before he knew what he was doing, Carlyon said that he would go to find the flowers for her. She put her hands on the table and almost jumped to her feet in her excitement. It was as if she were about to leap and throw her arms around his neck, and if she had, he would have thought himself adequately compensated. Her father looked at her and shook his head, almost as if in disbelief. John's reaction was to laugh, but he said nothing. Carlyon also said no more. He had spoken on impulse, but it could not be withdrawn. A vow had been made and could not now be broken. He knew that if he decided not to undertake the search, Patrina would never marry him.

# 4

As those who were left in the great hall began to get up from the table, Carlyon left his seat and went over to the fireplace. The minstrel had finished off his ale and was gathering up his things, before going to see where he would be sleeping that night. Carlyon stood with his back to what was left of the fire and told the minstrel that he had given a fine performance. The man thanked him humbly and looked at him expectantly. Carlyon realised that the man thought that he was about to get a few extra coins, and he felt a pang of dismay that he had left his purse in his bedchamber, not having foreseen any need for it. He pushed aside such thoughts, as if they were irritating flies. He needed information from the man.

"I was interested in your final song – the one about the flowers of the swan. Is the tale true? Does it really happen?"

The minstrel looked at him shrewdly, as if estimating what profit there would be for him. "It's an ancient legend, sir. I've not seen it myself, but I've heard of men who have."

"Where does it happen? Where do the swans go to die?"

"I've heard it said they fly north-westwards to a forest. They sing their song there and then they die. Do you mean to seek the flowers for the lady?"

"Yes. Can you tell me more clearly where this place is?"

The minstrel licked his lips and pondered. He then spoke as if he had come to a decision. "I can't tell you that. I've heard it's beyond the city of Chester, in a place between two rivers. Mayhap, sir, if you were to travel to those parts and watch for a flying swan, you would be lucky."

"Mayhap so. It seems I have no other choice."

Carlyon let out his breath sharply and began to move round the minstrel to leave. As he did so, he told the man to come and see him on the morrow before he left. The minstrel nodded respectfully, and the next morning he presented himself to Carlyon shortly after breakfast. Ready for him this time, Carlyon gave him a few coins in thanks for the information he had given to him, limited though it had been. They were given ruefully, but without rancour, because although in the cold light of that November day Carlyon was worried about what the man had unintentionally got him into, he accepted that it would be unfair to blame him.

The minstrel took the money with grateful thanks and prepared to walk away, but then, as if suddenly recalling something to mind, he stopped. "Do you still mean to seek the flowers of the swan, sir?"

"That's my intention."

"The place where the flowers are to be found is said to be dangerous, protected by magic. You must prepare yourself well before you set off on this journey. When you are ready, take some corn to be blessed by a holy man. Then go to a river where there are swans and scatter the corn for them to eat. This will bring you luck and help to protect you on your journey."

"I'll do that. And that will protect me when I pick the flowers?"

"I know not, sir. Men say there will be a curse on whoever picks the flowers."

Carlyon's eyes widened. He had been pleased to hear about the blessed corn, but now there was something else. He drew in a quick breath and expelled it forcefully, unsure what to do. "Is there any way of averting this curse?" he asked doubtfully.

"All curses can be averted. Also this one. But I know not how. You'll need to seek farther." The minstrel looked at Carlyon as if he felt sorry for him, and turned to walk away.

Left by himself, Carlyon stood in thought for several seconds, but found nothing as his mind hummed in twists and turns. To get some relief, he walked up and down the room a few times, but still he found nothing clear, no definite way forward. He was interrupted by John, who called to him from the doorway to remind him that the hunt was almost ready to leave. It seemed that John had forgotten Carlyon's rash pledge of the previous night, because he mentioned nothing of it.

However, Patrina had well remembered, and she spoke of it when they met. "When will you be leaving on your travels for me, Sir Carlyon?"

The bluntness of the question made him move his head back, as if she had thrown it into his face. However, he replied phlegmatically. "I'll need to make arrangements. There are many things to prepare, but I hope to be setting off by the month's end."

"Do you know where to find the flowers? I pray your absence won't be a long one. I'm dying to see these flowers."

"I also pray my task will soon be completed. I intend to seek in the north. There's wild, deserted country there."

"Oh, Sir Carlyon! I hope it won't be too dangerous."

She gave a delightful shiver, which sent a corresponding tremble through Carlyon's chest. He smiled at her and pressed his advantage.

"Who knows what dangers will lie there? But I'll face them for you, my lady, and God willing, I'll return in triumph."

To help him, the following day he spoke to the earl for advice about travelling to the north-west of England. The earl seemed surprised that Carlyon was continuing to indulge his daughter's whimsy, and chaffed him good-humouredly. Carlyon's initial feeling was one of pleasure, and he joined in with the earl's laughter. A thought had come to him that the earl would say that he wanted him to marry Patrina. In that case, the search could be forgotten. However, the earl said nothing of that.

"I ween you're young enough for such adventures. A few weeks of absence will do you no harm. 'Sblood! You'll be back before we know you've left us. So, you want to know about the north country? Speak to old Christopher. He was in service under my father on my manor in Lancashire. He'll tell you about that part of the land, I'll warrant."

One day at the end of November, Carlyon was in his chamber when John came to see him. His preparations were well advanced. He had taken some corn to a nearby priory and had it blessed by the abbot, who had a reputation for holiness, and he was gathering the clothing that he would be taking. John, after dismissing the boy who had carried the goblets and the flagon of wine for him, examined Carlyon's armour with a critical eye. Carlyon poured out some wine and waited for his friend's comment. The armour, however, seemed satisfactory, because John left it and reached for his wine.

"Pray God you don't need the armour, but best to have it," he said. "What else? It's going to be cold. And I have heard it can be very bitter in those northern parts."

"I'm taking plenty of warm clothing." Carlyon indicated the woollen breeches, the tunics and the surtouts. "I'll have three cloaks."

"How long will you be away?"

"Perhaps three months, so I doubt. I'll be back before Candlemas."

"Do you know where you're going? Where are these flowers?"

"I've spoken to old Christopher. He knows the area well. He's never heard of a place where the swans go to die, but he thinks the likeliest place to begin the search would be somewhere called the Forest of Wirral."

"I've never heard of that. Is it a far-distant place?"

"Not so distant, I think. Christopher has told me how to get there."

John nodded, seemingly satisfied with the preparations. He reached over and picked up Carlyon's sword in its scabbard. "Is this the one you're taking?"

Carlyon inclined his head in affirmation.

"You may need it. I fear there'll be fierce beasts in this forest." John looked straight at Carlyon and said gravely, "I pray God will guard you and bring you back safely."

"Thank you, John." Carlyon was touched by his friend's sincere wishes. He knew that they were rivals in many things, but he also knew that they had a strong friendship. "I pray also that I'll return safely and successfully to claim the lady Patrina's hand."

"Hah! We'll see, we'll see. When do you plan to leave?"

"Tuesday morning. At dawn."

"Good. I'll come to see you away."

When Carlyon told Patrina of his departure date, he could almost see the excitement which bubbled into her breast and made her arms flutter. She was unable to keep still.

"How marvellous!" she cried, pulling in her mouth to push up her cheekbones, and hunching her shoulders in her pleasure. "Oh, it'll be so lovely when you come back. I'll come down to see you leave. I have a ring for you. It was given to me by my grandmother and I've been told it has magical properties. It'll help to keep you safe from evil on your journey."

Joy at Patrina's words raced through him like a flame, and his face brightened as if a light were shining on it. If they had been alone, he would have embraced her. But Patrina seemed not to notice how his love for her was raising him upwards, as she continued to talk excitedly about his forthcoming adventure. Then she bethought herself and looked at him kindly.

"You will take care of yourself, won't you? I don't know how I'll be able to wait until your return, thinking about you. I wonder what adventures you'll have. There'll be so many tales you'll have to tell me. And you'll be doing it all for me. You will carry the flowers carefully, won't you? Do you think they'll be as beautiful as they sound?"

"I'm sure they will. But not so beautiful as you."

He spoke those words in an attempt to get her attention back on him, and he had some success, although excitement still seemed to be pushing her mind beyond him. Even so, Carlyon was not unhappy. He sensed that he would always be a presence in her thoughts.

During the following Monday night there was a frost. It was not severe, as it was only early December, but there was a piercing chill in the air when James brought a candle into Carlyon's chamber and woke him. Carlyon got out of bed reluctantly, but once he was moving, he began to feel better. He poured hot water into a bowl from a jug which a page had brought in, and thankfully washed his face and hands. His clothes had been laid out ready and he dressed quickly, the initial coldness of the fabrics soon becoming comfortable on contact with his body. When he was fully dressed, he knelt and said a brief prayer.

Downstairs there was already a fire in the great hall, and he warmed himself by it before sitting down to a breakfast of bread, cold meat and ale. He was joined in his meal by John, who was in an excellent mood for so early in the morning.

"How now, Carlyon?" he boomed from the doorway. "Are we ready?"

"As ready as I can be." Carlyon's reply was lacking in heartiness, but he smiled at his friend. He was pleased to have company and it helped to lighten his feelings at having to go away.

"Are you sure you have all you need?" John asked as he began to eat.

Carlyon was touched by the note of genuine concern in John's voice, and he confirmed immediately that all his preparations were complete. He continued with his meal, and John's bluff conversation was a welcome warmth around them. Even so, Carlyon was impelled by restlessness, and constantly glanced over at the doorway.

Eventually John noticed. "What's amiss? You seem to be on the watch."

"Forgive me, John. Lady Patrina said she would come to wish me farewell. I hoped she would join us at breakfast."

"Ha, ha! Not she, I ween. She likes her bed too much."

"Mayhap that be so. Well, she'll just be coming to the courtyard to see me off." Carlyon nodded in acceptance to hide his disappointment, and finished his meal.

Then, as the first grey clouds of light were sneaking over the horizon, he and John went outside. James was already there. Champion was stamping loudly on the cobbles, snorting steam through his nostrils, and he whinnied when he saw Carlyon, as if he knew that they would soon be on their way. James was making final adjustments at the packhorse, which was laden with panniers, into which he had packed Carlyon's armour and the other things that they would need on their journey. Carlyon blew out his breath, so that he could see the water vapour, and suddenly wished that he was back in bed and need not leave on his search.

John seemingly had no such thoughts. He spoke cheerily. "This is it. You must be on your way now. Dawn's broken. By Christ's blood, I wish I was going with you. It'll be an adventure. We two could achieve anything."

"I also wish you were coming. But I've got to do this on my own." Carlyon broke off as someone appeared in the doorway, but the sudden leap of joy in his breast was knocked down when he saw that it was only the young page whom he had sent to enquire after Patrina. "Is my lady coming?" he asked.

"No, sir. I spoke to her maid. She said that her lady is still abed. She said that she woke her lady before dawn, but she said it was cold. She's gone back to sleep, but she did send her good wishes."

John laughed outright, as if imagining Patrina in bed, but Carlyon set his face grimly and asked if Lady Patrina had sent a ring for him. The boy shook his head and said that the maid had given him nothing. Carlyon nodded, but still hid his disappointment. He reached to put a hand on Champion's bridle, but before he could mount, John spoke.

"Here a moment, Carlyon." He clicked his fingers and a servant stepped away from the wall to hand him a shield. "I've got something for you. This has been a good protector to me and I hope it'll be the same to you."

As he took the shield from John, Carlyon looked at it, caught by the unexpected gesture. It seemed nothing special. It was simply made of a dull metal with a black boss in the centre, but Carlyon hefted it in both hands and found it surprisingly light. "Thank you, John," he said. "I'll take care of it and I pray it'll take care of me."

He hung the shield from his saddle and turned back to John. The two men embraced warmly and then broke away.

"Godspeed!" said John, as Carlyon climbed onto Champion's back.

Carlyon acknowledged the blessing with a wave and set off, followed by James who was leading the packhorse. As they clopped over the courtyard, Carlyon turned his head slightly to look up at Patrina's window. Sadness slipped down into his breast like a leaden chain, but he hoped that she was at least dreaming of him. He did not know that, woken by the clatter of hooves on flagstones, she did pull herself out of bed to go to her window. Pushing back the shutter, she looked out for a few seconds, shivering in the cold air, but to her disappointment her knight and his squire were already out of sight and she went back to her bed.

Carlyon's thoughts dwelt only on his lady love. As his horse plodded along the highway, he pulled his travelling cloak around him, nestling his chin into the fur collar. It was fully daylight, but the sun was not yet high enough to counter the chill of the wind or melt the frost that had candied the branches of the trees. Thinking about Patrina kept his mind occupied and helped to keep him warm. It was easy to make excuses for her non-appearance. She had spoken fondly to him at supper the previous night. She was clearly excited at the prospect of being gifted the flowers of the swan. It was very cold that morning. Even he had been reluctant to leave his bed. It would have been good if she had come to see him off, but he could at least think of the warm welcome that he would receive on his triumphant return.

Despite his efforts, sadness was a heavy log across his shoulders for much of the morning and, lost in his thoughts, he was barely aware of the road they were taking. By noontime, however, he was riding alongside James and the pair of them were talking freely. When they stopped for dinner, Carlyon was glad of the chance to stretch his legs and to allow Champion to rest. There was still hazy sunshine and it was having a pleasant effect on his mood. After dismounting, he cheerily stroked Champion's neck and began to loosen the girth. Then he saw his bag, partly hidden by John's shield, hanging from the saddle, and he stopped short, his breath hot in his mouth. He knew that there was no point in reaching into the bag. He knew what he would find there.

"James!" he called over to where his squire was dealing with the other two horses. "I forgot to scatter the corn."

"Sire?"

"I have some corn which was blessed by Father Bernard, and I should have fed it to the swans on the river when we set off this morning. It was to bring us good luck, but I was so busy thinking about something else that I forgot."

"What are you going to do?"

48

"I don't know." Vexation tightened Carlyon's lips and he pulled thoughtfully at Champion's bridle as he pondered. "It's too late to go back now. We've come too far."

"Will we have bad luck if we don't?"

"I don't know. Perhaps we will. Oh, how could I have forgotten? I thought things were going so well."

"Shall I ride back quickly and do it? I can catch you again tomorrow."

"No. Your horse will be too tired. I'll keep the corn. It might come in useful. If we find some swans on our way, I'll scatter the corn for them. Pray God that will ward off any ill fortune."

Carlyon smiled optimistically at James, but when they set off again after their dinner, he was still worried about any possible consequences of his negligence. Their journey continued without incident, however, and in the evening they found a place to provide lodging and food also for their horses.

# 5

Somewhat refreshed, they set off again the following morning. They made good time through the Chiltern Hills and by early afternoon they were approaching Aylesbury, where they hoped to spend the night. Their road brought them out of a stand of beech trees and they came upon a field in which a man and a woman were ploughing. Carlyon observed them with interest as he rode towards them, because they seemed to be the only other figures in the landscape. The man was harnessed to the plough with a simple leather trace, and as he pulled it down the strip, the woman followed, pressing the plough into the soil. It had been a frosty day with little sunshine. The temperature was still not far above freezing point, and as he watched the shiny clay roll over onto its back, Carlyon could almost feel the effort the man was putting in to pull the plough through the hard ground.

Then Carlyon's attention was diverted. Their road led them along the side of the field. Now he saw three children waiting there. Two of them were girls, whom he judged to be between four and six years old. The third was an infant wrapped in rags in a rough wooden cradle. The girls, standing in their bare feet on the icy ground, had been crying in the chilly wind, but they fell silent to look at the two strangers riding towards them. Carlyon reined in Champion and looked at the tearful faces which were turned up to him. The girls wore dirty woollen shifts, and had an old sheet across their shoulders to give them some kind of protection from the weather. Carlyon wondered how long they had been standing there, waiting for their parents. Judging by what had been freshly ploughed, it was probably all day. He looked down kindly at the children, and sorrow for their suffering burned through his breast.

"A moment, James. I think I have something for these." As he spoke, he dismounted and went to the packhorse. From a pannier he pulled out an old fur cloak. Taking it to the children, who were looking at him with wide, almost fearful eyes, he put the cloak across their shoulders. "There, children. Pull it round you. That's right." He stepped back a pace and felt a sigh of satisfaction that they were small enough that the cloak covered them completely and skimmed the ground. "That's better, I'll warrant, is it not?"

Winking encouragingly at them, he then glanced at the cradle. However, the toddler was looking up and smiling, seemingly quite comfortable. Carlyon assumed that the cradle was giving shelter and that the rags were providing enough warmth. He looked back to the girls and asked them their names. He was intending to give them a penny, but before they could answer, there was a loud clanging noise from the field.

Turning his head sharply, he saw that the plough was on its side. The ploughman and his wife were struggling to free from the ground's sticky grasp the obstruction they had hit. Carlyon, watching curiously, heard James's horse move restlessly. He knew that his squire wanted to be on their way. After the uncomfortable night they had spent in the open, he would not want to miss their lodging and spend another such night. Nor did Carlyon, but his attention was drawn towards what was happening in the field.

The man and his wife worked together, moving lumps of soil and pulling at the object. Suddenly it was free and the man was holding a sword in his hands. Even from where he was, Carlyon could see that it was bright, despite having been in the ground, and he guessed that it would be easy to clean and polish up. The man looked over at him, and then said something to his wife. Then he started to come across, careless of the mud which he was collecting on his boots as he stepped over the newly ploughed furrows. His wife followed him, stepping more gingerly in her bare feet that had been cut by icy stones during the ploughing. Carlyon wondered at this kind of life; a life that he'd never seen before.

When the man reached Carlyon, he held out the sword to show him. "I've found this sword, sir. Would you like to look at it?"

Carlyon took it without a word, wiped his gloved left hand down the blade, and then hefted it in his right hand. There was no doubt that it was a good sword. The weight was excellent, as if it had been made to order for him. He tried out a few practice strokes and felt totally at ease with it. It was almost as if hand, gauntlet and grip had become fused together, so that the sword was an extension of his arm. He felt that he would be able to do wondrous things with such a weapon.

Slowly, he brought his arm to a stop and carefully lifted the sword to rest the flat of the blade on his clenched left fist. He looked at the faces of the man and his wife, who were looking at him with a mixture of humility and expectation. He realised that they were hoping that he would be so impressed by the sword that he would want to keep it. There was no question. He knew that he had to have the sword. Handing it up to James, he took off his glove and felt in the pouch beneath his tunic. He took out three gold coins and asked the man if he would take them in exchange for the sword. The man's wife poked his back in encouragement, but her husband was already reaching gratefully for the money. Carlyon told James to wrap the sword and put it away, and then looked back at the man.

"Why are you out ploughing on a day like this?" he asked.

"We've not been able to do it sooner, sir." The man, lacking a purse, had put the coins behind his child in the cradle for safekeeping. He now straightened up and flexed his spine. "We've been working these past weeks for my lady on the manor lands, and because of sickness we've only just been able to begin our own ploughing."

"Lucky for me that you were here today."

"Lucky for us also, sir, that you should be passing this way. Are you visiting nearby?"

Carlyon shook his head and looked at the man in his tattered clothes and with face and hands grimy from his toil. He was about to reach out for Champion's bridle, ready to mount, when impulse prodded him and he told the man that he was on a special journey. He was seeking the flowers of the swan. The man nodded, but Carlyon could tell that it meant nothing to him, so he told him about the legend. The man's face moved from politeness to interest, and he asked Carlyon where he was seeking the flowers.

"I know not. Know you where such are to be found?"

He had a strange feeling that he had been drawn to this spot so that he would be helped in his search, and he prepared to reach into his purse for another reward. However, the man scratched his head thoughtfully through his hood and then admitted that he had no idea. He looked at his wife, but she shook her head, unable to help. Disappointed, Carlyon turned towards Champion. As he did so, the sun broke unexpectedly through the lowering cloud.

A beam seemed to shine straight onto the toddler in the cradle, illuminating the child with a miraculous brightness that burned right into Carlyon's heart. As he looked, transfixed momentarily, the child pointed at him and then spoke.

"Not man."

Carlyon's brow furrowed, unsure about what he had heard. It seemed to mean nothing. He inhaled, but before he could say anything, the child spoke again.

"Girl hard."

Again Carlyon was unsure if he had heard aright. This time he asked the child what it had said. As he was speaking, the cloud covered the sun once more and the brightness disappeared. The child looked up at him and smiled, seeming not to understand the question.

"What did the babe say?" Carlyon asked the father. "What did it mean?"

"I don't know, sir. He's only just starting to talk. There, Sal, you understand his baby talk. What did he mean?"

Appealed to, the mother shook her head and said that he had never used such words before. She bent over the child, clucking her tongue and asking him what he had said. The child gurgled and smiled, but said nothing more. Carlyon sighed, shrugged, and gave a farthing for each of the children. Then he mounted Champion and he and James carried on towards Aylesbury without looking back.

When they reached the town, they found some lodgings at an inn not far from the church and Carlyon went to his room to relax and consider what had happened. The child's words still meant nothing to him, and after some fruitless thought, he was inclined to simply dismiss them as meaningless babbling. He was about to go downstairs for supper when there was a knock at his door. It was James. In his hands he held the sword which had been found in the field. He had wiped and polished it, and when the candlelight caught it as he moved into the room, sparkling glints of light seemed to run down the blade. Carlyon took it and examined it. The metal was of good quality. A master craftsman had fashioned it. The decoration on the haft was simple – an engraved swirl inlaid with a few precious stones – and Carlyon looked at it curiously, trying to guess its meaning. It seemed to be a secret sign, and he hoped that it would bring him good luck. He put his hand round the haft. It seemed to fit as if made for him, and as he swung it gently, he felt a warm tingle pass from the sword to his arm. He raised his head and looked at James with eyes that were glittering in triumph.

"My thanks to you, James. You've done well. I feel I'll be able to do wonders with this sword. It will always be part of me now."

He wrapped it again in the clean linen cloth that James had brought, and put it with his other things. Almost reluctantly, he then left and went downstairs for supper.

The inn's main room was not crowded, because there were few travellers at that time of year. Carlyon ordered their meals and the two of them went to sit by the fire with a mulled drink until called to table. It was pleasant there, and after the uncomfortable sleep which they had had the previous night, they both began to feel drowsy. Suddenly Carlyon realised that a woman was standing in front of him. Thinking that he was being called for his meal, he made to get to his feet. But the woman rested her fingertips lightly on his shoulder.

"One moment, Sir Knight," she said coldly.

Realising that she was not speaking like a servant, Carlyon mentally shook himself and looked at her closely. In the uncertain light he judged that she was of late middle age, and well dressed. Her woollen gown had a finely embroidered moulded bodice, which he could glimpse under her richly dyed supertunic. Her gown's skirt was cut wide and fell in folds to her feet, on which she wore fine leather shoes. Her hair was covered by a black veil, and a white wimple framed her long, thin face. Obviously she was a woman of substance, but it was her face which drew Carlyon's fascinated attention. The chin was long and pointy with a slight upward curve caused by the lack of teeth on the lower jaw. The hooked nose was moving towards the chin like a beak; the two of them seemingly held apart only by her thin lips and sallow cheeks. The eyes were dark and piercing and held Carlyon in a gaze that dried up the moisture in his throat. Before he could say anything, she spoke again, her voice authoritative but at the same time insinuating.

"You have a sword which was found by one of my tenants. The sword was found on my land and so I am the rightful owner. You must give it to me."

When she stopped speaking, she smiled, but Carlyon preferred it when she was looking fierce. She had a strange, frightening presence. Nervously he looked at her, and she lifted her hands, holding them out as if about to cup his face. The fingers were long and thin like knives, and he involuntarily moved his head backwards.

"You must give me the sword," she said softly. "It belongs to me. It's mine. I won't leave here without it."

Carlyon did not want to give up the sword, but he seemed unable to resist the woman. It was as if the two of them were alone.

He did not even notice how James was staring at them with his eyes wide in silent fear, as if he too was frightened by the woman. Carlyon was on his own. With a heavy heart pressing on his lungs, he breathlessly told the woman that he would go to his room and get the sword. He was unable to resist her, even though his leaden feet seemed to be walking through mire.

In his room he took out the woman's sword and unwrapped it. Then he stopped, held firm by a sense that he should not give it away. As he contemplated it, the blade glittered as before in the candlelight. Regret trembled down his arms and made the sword quiver. The glittering became more active, as if agitated, and then died away. He sighed sadly in his helplessness and began to rewrap the sword. While he was doing so, he glanced at the shield which John had given him. He had leaned it against the wall, and as he looked at it, he saw that shadows had transformed the boss into a face. He plainly saw eyes, a nose and a mouth, and, staring through the dimness, he thought that he saw the lips move. Momentarily he clenched his eyes closed and twitched his head slightly. He looked again, trying to focus intently. Again he saw the lips move, and this time he also seemed to hear a voice: low and sonorously deep, but perfectly clear in his ears.

"Beware of the woman," it told him. "She is a witch."

Carlyon was held as if unable to move, his eyes transfixed on the face which he could see on the shield. His tongue pressed against the backs of his teeth, and he was incapable of speech. When the voice continued after a brief pause, as if having ensured that it had Carlyon's attention, he could only listen.

"That woman is the Evil One. She wants the sword so that she can do evil with it. You must not give it to her. You will need it, and you will be able to do good with it. It has mighty power. In evil hands it can do great evil, but in the hands of a good man it will only do wondrous good."

The words seemed to act like a prod. Carlyon moved his head and found that he could speak. "The sword. Yes. I must keep it. But she is demanding it." He looked away, and almost immediately it came to him. "I can give her my sword. That may do."

"The woman will not expect you to trick her. When you have given her the sword and she has left, you also must leave straight away. You have a task to complete. The love of a good woman is awaiting you."

"Yes. We must be away before the old woman discovers the trick."

Carlyon had lowered his gaze while he said those last few words. When he looked again at the shield, the shadows on the boss had smoothed themselves out. He furrowed his brow and reached out with his free hand to touch the shield. It was smooth and clean as it had always been. Straightening up, he looked at the sword in his hand and wondered if he had imagined it all. Of course. Perhaps it had been the mulled ale? The shadows had played tricks with his eyes. And his ears.

There was no time to wonder more. He had a sword and the woman was waiting for him downstairs. Moving decisively, he took his own sword out of its scabbard and replaced it carefully with the new one. As he did so, it seemed to pull itself in and he thought he saw it flash briefly. Wasting no more time, he wrapped his old sword in the cloth and tied it tightly with a cord. For a second he looked at it, and then he went downstairs.

The woman was waiting, standing by the fireplace, as if she had not moved while he had been away. When he gave her the sword, she clutched it with a gasp of satisfaction and put it into a box which she had with her. There were no more words, not even of thanks. The woman acted as though she could no longer see Carlyon or anyone else. She left, and it seemed to Carlyon that the room was suddenly warmer. He turned to James, but before he could speak, their meals were brought in. He decided to wait. They would eat first before leaving. It would give time for the woman to get away, so that she would not see them leave.

Carlyon had not realised how hungry he was, and when he joined the few other guests who were already eating at the inn's long table, he ate heartily. While he did so, he told James that they were going to leave immediately after the meal. James expressed surprise that they would be travelling after dark, and asked why. Carlyon paused with a piece of cheese on his knife, about to put it in his mouth. He thought it best not to say anything about the voice he had imagined.

"I liked not that woman," he said. "I think she may mean us mischief. I kept the sword she wanted, and gave her my old one. So we ought to leave before she finds out." He ignored James's wide eyes and resumed eating.

"Where will we go?" James asked.

"Oxford. There's a good moon this night. We should be able to get there by midnight and we'll find lodgings there without trouble. We'll be safe there," Carlyon added, wanting to reassure his young companion.

Carlyon did not want to talk about the woman any more, as he was worried about what would happen when she discovered his deception. There was an awkward tickling in his stomach, but he made an effort not to show any unease to James. Forcing calmness into his voice, he began to discuss how long it would take to get their horses ready, and said he hoped that the animals would not be too tired. Their supper was quickly finished and, after drinking down the last of his ale, Carlyon told James that they should be getting ready to leave. To his surprise, he saw that James was looking at him with heavy eyes, as if on the point of falling asleep. Carlyon was about to chivvy him, when James's mouth opened in a huge yawn. Despite himself, Carlyon joined him, and suddenly he began to feel an almost overwhelming desire to sleep, to rest. No, he told himself firmly. I mustn't sleep. It's too warm in here. We'll be fine when we're out in the fresh air. That'll keep us awake.

Pushing against the heavy cords which seemed to be holding him down, Carlyon got to his feet and pulled at James's shoulder to get him up off the bench. "Get your things together," he told him, "and go out to the horses."

Together they went to the stairs and stumbled up to their rooms. Inside his, Carlyon looked at his travelling pouch and then picked up his outdoor boots. It was as if someone else were doing those things, but he forced himself to sit on the bed and put the boots on the floor beside him. He kept his hand on one, ready to put it on his foot, but his sleepiness seemed to be pressing him backwards with inexorable hands. It was almost overpowering, but he thought that if he just lay on the bed for a minute or two, then he would recover his breath. He was barely able to lie back and lift up his feet before his eyes closed and he became insensible; all thoughts of the witch lost in a black emptiness.

# 6

When Carlyon woke up, it was still dark outside, but there were sounds of activity from the inn's servants downstairs and in the yard. For a while he lay dreaming on the bed. He had no recollection of where he was or why. Nor was he able to understand why his mouth was dry and his head was aching. He was also feeling cold, and was surprised to find himself lying fully clothed on a bed, after a sleep which had been so deep that he had not been bothered by the lice and fleas.

Suddenly he remembered that he was at an inn, and that he had to leave. He jerked himself upright. As he did so, fiery bands tightened round his head. Pressing it with both hands, he swung his legs over the side of the bed and tried to draw in a deep breath. His head felt fuzzy and his balance was shaky, but he got to his feet. Furrowing his brow, he wondered how he could have got so drunk – and James seemingly also. He had surely not had more than a quart. What kind of ale were they brewing in Aylesbury?

In the darkness, he staggered over to the door of his room. He opened it and called for a light. Answered, he turned back and felt his way over to the table. The jug of water there was cold; icy to the touch. Almost thankfully, he lifted it and took a swig. Then, pouring some into the bowl, he splashed his face and washed his hands. He was just drying himself when a boy came in with a light and asked him if he wanted hot water.

"No! No time for that. Wake my squire and have our horses made ready. And tell the landlord I'll want the reckoning. I'll be down directly."

Urgently, he gathered up his things and went downstairs. Bread and some small beer were already waiting, but Carlyon was more pleased to see a fire roaring in the grate. He stood near it while he ate, and although he looked dubiously at the ale, he drank it and seemed none the worse. In fact his head was now almost clear, and when the landlord came into the room to tell him that his horses were ready, he nodded his satisfaction with no ill effect. The landlord had prepared the bill the previous night and, after a small adjustment, Carlyon paid it while James was finishing off his breakfast.

"I'm glad you decided to stay, sir," said the landlord. "I hope you were comfortable."

"I've been severely delayed," Carlyon replied, ignoring the landlord's unctuous tone and still putting the blame for the delay on his ale.

"I'm sorry about that, sir. I didn't know. Where are you going?"

"We're going to Oxford. Important business. I must be away now."

Picking up his sword and shield and his pouch, Carlyon walked towards the door. James, who had needed no telling to gather up the rest of their things, followed immediately. By the light of a torch held by a stablehand, they checked their horses and then mounted. Carlyon led the way slowly out of the inn yard and turned down the street. Dawn was still almost an hour away and few people were yet about their business, so their departure was observed by no one of consequence. Those who did, saw them take the Oxford road.

Once clear of the town limits, Carlyon quickened his pace for two or three miles, but as greyness began to make it easier for him to make out landmarks, he looked around him. Eventually he seemed to see what he was seeking when they came to a crossroads in a small hamlet. He halted there, looked back the way they had come, and then took the road to the right.

"Is this the road to Oxford?" asked James, screwing up his face in his uncertainty.

"No. We're not going to Oxford. If we're searched for, let them search there. This road will take us to Bicester and get us back onto our proper way. When we get to Warwick, we'll find a river. I'm sure there'll be swans there and I'll be able to feed them with my corn."

Carlyon furrowed his brow, but looked straight ahead. He did not want to show James how worried he was at their delay; nor why he felt that deception was necessary.

They took their dinner in Banbury, but did not tarry long. In fact Carlyon would not have stopped at all, except that he wanted to rest the horses. He had a feeling that he would need to keep them fresh. When they set off again, they were riding into an icy north-west wind which, despite their thick cloaks, seemed to cut through into their flesh with steel-cold sharpness. Clouds were blown up in front of them, and before long they were travelling through sleet. Conditions became bitterly uncomfortable. Again Carlyon wondered how he had got himself into this position, but he knew that they had to press on. At least other travellers were seldom met with, and those they did encounter passed by as if in a hurry to reach their destination.

It was with warm gratitude and a sincere prayer of thankfulness that at last Carlyon saw the spire of Coventry Cathedral in the distance. Champion also seemed to sense that their day's journey was close to an end, because he responded willingly when his master spurred him to a faster pace. They stopped at the first inn they came upon and, after seeing the horses settled in the stable, hurried into the warmth of the inn. There they found that mulled wine was already awaiting them in front of a roaring fire.

Later that evening, after he had thawed out and had an excellent supper, Carlyon was in his room, listening to the sleet on his shutter and pondering over his next move. The thought came into his mind that perhaps he should have given the witch her sword and not tried to trick her just because he had imagined hearing a voice and seeing a face. The wind was howling outside. The icy rain rapped insistently at his window. It was as if dark spirits were wanting to get in to him. Suppose the witch was even now riding on the storm, flying about outside, waiting for him to fall asleep alone in his room? Involuntarily he looked at the shutter and wondered how stout it was. Then he looked at his candle, fluttering occasionally as a draught caught it. He could not stop himself from wondering how long it would last.

Glumly he shook his head and wished that he was back at Chertsey, or even at his father's house. Things were not going to plan. Because the weather had been so bad that afternoon, they had not travelled via Warwick, but even if they had, he doubted that under such conditions they would have found swans swimming on the Avon. So once again he had been unable to scatter his corn. He sighed. The journey, having been begun, must be completed. He could not return without something to show for it, for if he did, Lady Patrina would not be the only one to despise him.

While he was sitting there, toying with weariness as if it were a rosary passing through his fingers, his gaze alighted on the shield. It was resting against his saddle pouch, next to his sword, and as he looked, it appeared to shake slightly. Something seemed to be holding his head and he was unable to move his gaze away. Gradually he saw the shield's boss take on human features, just as it had the previous night. He waited one second; two. Then the shield began to speak, its voice again low and sonorously deep in Carlyon's ears.

"You have been foolish. You did not do what you should have. You should not have spent the night in Aylesbury."

"I didn't mean to stay. Something made me sleep."

"A sleeping draught had been put into the ale which you drank. This is not good. The witch has discovered your deception and she is about to set off in pursuit of you. The landlord of the inn will send her to Oxford and she will spend fruitless time there."

"We'll leave straight away."

"No. You will be safe tonight."

"Yes. We must rest. Mayhap the storm will have blown out by morning. But where should we go from here?"

"The child told you where to go. Follow his instructions."

"His words were beyond my understanding. 'Not man.' What does that mean? I can make no sense of it."

"The child told you to go to Nottingham."

"Of course – I understand that now! But what about 'girl hard'?"

"When you get to Nottingham, you must seek out a goliard."

"I see clearly now. Yes. This goliard will help me. We must lose no time." Emboldened by what he had understood, Carlyon looked intently at the shield. "Who are you? Where are you from? What magic is this?"

There was no reply. As if he had blinked, he saw that there was no longer a face on the shield. He looked at it closely. The smooth, featureless boss looked back at him. He turned it over to examine the back. He blew on the boss, but there was nothing. Almost nervously, he turned his head to look over his shoulder, but there was nobody else in the room. He could hear nothing but the weather outside. It was as if he had imagined it all.

He wondered if there had been a potion in his drink which had made his fancies run wild. Could that be? He shook his head. There was no reason for that to have happened. Perhaps he had truly seen a face and heard a voice? But it was surely not evil? It must be a good spirit sent from God; a guardian angel, perhaps. He nodded. There was no help for it now. At least he knew what to do, and on the morrow he would hasten on his journey. He pulled in his lips firmly as he sat in thought. He must not linger. Lady Patrina was waiting for him and he knew that she would not wait forever for her knightly love.

He closed his eyes in a brief prayer and then got to his feet. Thoughtfully, he went over to the window and checked the shutter. Turning, he looked around the room. He was alone. He exhaled sharply and began to prepare for bed. Beneath his blanket, he lay and thought over what he would find at Nottingham. By now he was feeling hopeful, because he believed that the shield would help him and that he would get some success there. When he fell asleep, his mood was greatly improved, but when he dreamed, it was an unsatisfying one about Lady Patrina.

## 7

*L*ady Patrina's father was holding an Advent ball. It was a great occasion, having been several days in preparation. Patrina had hoped that Carlyon would stay for it and leave on his search for the flowers of the swan after it, but she had not felt it proper to say that to him. He would be sorry to have missed it, she thought. He would have been sure to pay her much attention. She would have been the centre of attraction.

On the day of the ball itself, Patrina rose late and, after taking a bath, spent some time deciding what clothes she would wear. While her maid helped her to dress, she continued to dream about the imminent festivities. Some of the guests had come from as far away as London. It would be a grand affair. She was sure that many people would be interested in her. It was already known that a knight had gone on a mission for her. Men would wish that they could do the same and ladies would be jealous. She almost hugged herself in her delight.

When she went downstairs to the great hall, it was already crowded with guests, some of whom had arrived during the preceding days. Musicians were playing in the gallery – fiddles, flutes, shawms and other instruments – but the music was being provided as a backdrop. It was continuous, but not intrusive, so conversation was not hindered.

Patrina wandered around, observing what other ladies were wearing and exchanging greetings with people. She was soon in a huddle with two close friends at the side of the hall. The three of them were in high spirits, and giggled as they discussed the clothing of some of the older ladies. Then they began to speak about other guests. Before long one of Patrina's friends spoke admiringly about Sir John le Cerre-nore.

"Is he not handsome? See how his tunic fits round his chest. He's such a well-built man. I hear he's a valiant fighter on the tournament field."

"Yes, I've seen him there," said Patrina. Knowing, as her friend did not, that John had expressed a desire to marry her, she spoke proprietorially. "He fights like a true knight. He'd do valiant deeds for his lady, I'm sure."

"I wish I had such a knight. My father intends to marry me to an old friend of his in Kent."

"*Marriage?*" said Patrina, almost feeling jealous. "I'd like to marry, I think. It'll be lovely to be the mistress of your own house. To be able to do things without asking your father's permission."

"But you'd have another lord," said her second friend. "Surely you would do what your husband decreed?"

"Not I! My husband would be so enamoured of me that he would worship me and do everything I commanded. I'd be his lady above all, and his life, his heart, would be devoted to serving me." Patrina spoke almost dismissively, as if it were self-evident. It was something that she had often thought about. She wanted it to be true, but she did not hear what her friends thought of her view.

Before either could comment, they were interrupted by the earl's steward calling everyone to eat. The three of them went merrily together to the table and picked as they wished from the many different courses that had been provided. It was a leisurely meal. Towards the end of it, one of Patrina's friends leaned over and spoke excitedly to the other two.

"I've been watching Sir John le Cerre-nore. He's just over there. He keeps looking at me. I'm sure he's interested in me. I don't know what I'll do if he comes to talk to me."

The other two looked at John, but he was helping himself to a large serving of junket and seemed unaware that he was an object of interest.

"Was he looking at you?" asked Patrina, somewhat sharply. "He may have been looking at Julia. Or even at me." She said that last as if it was of no interest to her at whom Sir John looked. She had, in fact, already noticed his glances and had been sure that they were directed at her. Occasionally she had wondered whether to acknowledge him, but propriety had held her back. She did not need to encourage him. Now she looked with a smile at her friend, who answered immediately.

"Oh no, Patsy, I'm certain he was looking at me. I could tell."

"Humph. We'll see."

They did not have long to wait. Openly they watched as John lifted his bowl to his lips and took a few mouthfuls. When he laid the bowl down, he glanced over at the three ladies. He was far enough away for each one to think that he was looking straight at her, but it was Patrina, in the centre, who reacted first. She smiled and inclined her head slightly in acknowledgement. John grinned and went back to his pudding. Satisfied, Patrina reached for some cheese and felt no need to comment. Her friends might think that they were an object of attention, but she had proved the truth to herself. Sir John was still in love with her.

Later on, when the dancing was under way, Patrina noticed that John always contrived to be near her in the chain or the ring. As she danced and sang, she rewarded his endeavour with smiles and trembled in her happiness at feeling her power. When she went to rest, she sat demurely by her aunt, and sure enough, John came over. He bowed first to the elder lady, who accepted his polite homage with a non-committal nod. Then he simply stood in front of them with his arms akimbo, his head slightly back and his chin thrust forward. Patrina looked at him, and irritation at the arrogance of his smiling face ran down her body like hot sand. Two can play at that game, she thought.

"Well, Sir John," she said coolly, "I wonder how your friend Sir Carlyon is this day. He's often in my thoughts, as I wonder how he's succeeding in the task which he has so gallantly undertaken for me." She observed closely, but when John relaxed and then merely continued to smile without speaking, disappointment made her bite her lip. "I wish I knew where he was," she said, deliberately wistful.

"He'll be many miles from here, my lady. Perhaps he's fighting wild beasts or finding his way through trackless forests."

"Think you so?" she asked, discarding her attempt to tease. "Will he be safe?"

"Of course. He's a brave and fearless knight. I've known him since we were boys together. There's none braver, but for me. He'll fight any obstacle and I'm sure he'll overcome. "

"I'm glad you think he'll be safe, because he's facing all those dangers just for me."

"Nor would I shirk at danger. I would lay down my life to protect you. I wouldn't go away and leave you to face who knows what peril. I would be at your side with my strong right arm, ready to defend you, whatever should arise."

Her eyes widened in bright excitement as she asked, "Do you think I may run into danger?"

"Who knows what peril may assail you before Sir Carlyon returns? But you need have no fear. Before he left, he asked me to protect you while he's away."

"Truly?" She believed his lie, and hugged herself in her delight at being so important to two men. "That's so kind of you, and so thoughtful of him. Oh, I do so hope he fulfils his promise and returns quickly."

"I also, my lady. But I fear he's taken on a difficult task. Truly, he might fail, or he may take a long time, perhaps many years, before he returns to claim your hand in marriage."

"Oh, I hope not. I wouldn't want to wait for years. What would I do?"

"I hope you would scarce have to wait so long before your knight can carry you away on his mighty charger. I'm here and I wouldn't keep you waiting."

She swiftly jerked her head to look at him, abruptly brought down to earth and out of her dreamy cloud. It was as if she was seeing him for the first time. "Oh, Sir John," she said in regretful sweetness, "I can't be unfaithful to Sir Carlyon. I vowed to make no decision until he completes his search. He's trusting me to wait for his return."

"Of course he is, and nor would I ask you to break your pledge to my friend. Even so, my lady, you need to consider that he may not return for some time, or perhaps not at all. How long will you wait before you accept another faithful heart, which is also waiting? How long will your father wait?"

"I don't know. I hadn't thought. This is so vexatious. I fear it's becoming complicated."

"I can make it easier for you, my lady. You must set a date for his return, so you'll know how long you'll have to wait."

"Think you so? I'm not sure. How long could it be? Perhaps I ought to wait a little longer before considering that?"

"And then a little longer. So it'll go on. How long should it take to gather a few flowers? Not more than a few weeks. A month or so. Say he'll return by New Year's Day?"

"That seems too soon, Sir John." Fear at having to make a decision so quickly sent an icy tremor to shake her heart. "I'm sure it ought to be later. I would fain not miss him by a few days."

"Of course. Candlemas would be a more suitable date. Say you'll wait until then, and if he has not returned, then you'll marry me."

"I can't make that decision yet. It still seems so soon. Ah, me! Why is it so difficult?"

"It's not *so* difficult. Here am I before you, offering a love that has no bounds. Say that Sir Carlyon must return before Easter. I too will not wait forever."

"Sir John! Easter? Perhaps. I scarcely know. It's hard to think with all this noise. Leave me now. I don't wish to talk about this any more today."

John looked at her narrowly, but then he bowed and moved away. Patrina watched him go almost with regret; her face drawn

72

into a mask of unresolved doubt. Her aunt looked at her and then remarked, as if inconsequentially, that Sir John was a handsome young man.

"He *is* handsome, Aunt, is he not? And brave. And dashing. He'd make a wonderful husband, I ween."

"For you?"

"He would. But he won't stay if I break his heart. I don't know what to do. Alas, why do I have to choose between the two of them?" She sighed, and petulance tightened her lips while she looked unheedingly at the rushes spread on the floor in front of her. "I wish Sir Carlyon would return soon – with my flowers."

Carlyon was in Nottingham. He and James had found lodgings at an inn under the Castle Rock. The day after their arrival, Carlyon walked around the cramped city, looking for a goliard. He had no idea what the man he sought might look like or where he was likely to be found. He went down this street and up that one, stepping round the piles of dung and other refuse that littered his path; in his absorption oblivious to the clinging odours around him. It seemed a hopeless task. The people he saw were no more than citizens and country folk going about their ordinary business. He was only thankful that the weather was dry. In the late afternoon, as dusk was falling, he returned to his lodgings. There he met up with James, who had also been out seeking and returned fruitless.

"Think you a goliard will help us?" asked James, as they sat together over glasses of mulled wine.

"Yes. I need to find a particular one and he will help me."

"How do you know which one?"

"We'll know which one," Carlyon said thoughtfully. "If only we can find one."

"I was talking to a woman selling bread and she said she'd seen no goliard in Nottingham since before Michaelmas. It's not the weather for wandering around."

"You may be right. And yet there must be one here. We must keep seeking."

Later that evening, after supper, they were sitting by the fire to sup some of the local ale. The room was crowded and noisy, but Carlyon was lost in his own thoughts. He gave a jerk when James tugged gently at his sleeve.

"Look over there, sire," he hissed excitedly. "That's Roderick Hoseford, the outlaw. I'm sure of it. Do you see?"

When Carlyon looked through the crowd, he saw that there was no doubt about it. It was Roderick, about whom there had been a hue and cry during that summer's tourney. And at least two of his band were drinking with him at the table.

"He has not been discovered yet, it seems," said James.

"So it is. Ah, me, it's none of our business. We can let the man be."

Nevertheless, Carlyon continued to look at him for a few seconds, and before he looked away, Roderick moved his head. Instantly, their eyes met. The laugh which was on Roderick's face following some merry quip with his men froze and seemed to slide off his chin. Carlyon saw that he too had been recognised, and he calmly nodded an acknowledgement to the outlaw. Roderick hurriedly said something to his companions and got to his feet. Carlyon thought that he was leaving, but instead he came over to sit beside him.

"Good even, Sir Knight. I little thought to see you in here."

"Nor I you, Master Hoseford. Are you seeking business here?"

"No. Simply a little warmth. And you? What business keeps you in Nottingham? Are you going to call the sheriff's men?"

"Not on this occasion." Carlyon smiled. "It's no matter to me what you do. I'm seeking a goliard. That's all I desire." He sighed and looked wearily at Roderick, as if bored with his presence. Then, on an impulse, he told him about the flowers of the swan which he was seeking.

"That's an odd business," mused Roderick. "It may be that there is a goliard in the city. But I'll leave you now to your search. My thanks for your forbearance, Sir Knight. May God keep you in his care." He bowed slightly as he got to his feet. Without another word, he swiftly left the inn, followed by his two men.

Carlyon shrugged and dismissed him from his mind.

Later that night, in his room, he picked up his shield and held it in his lap. Curiously, he examined it. First he turned it over and looked at the back; then the front. Eager thoughts rippled through his head. Was it magical? There seemed nothing out of the ordinary about it. Had it been blessed by a saint? Holding it with both hands, he hefted it briefly. It seemed to be only a shield. He wondered whether John knew about its power – if there *was* any such strange power. Perhaps that was why John had given him the shield: to help him achieve his task? Well, he needed help now.

He stared intently at the boss in the centre of the shield. For five, ten seconds he stared, but a boss it remained. Thinking that he was concentrating too hard, he half-closed his eyes and looked at the shield while trying to let his mind drift and see what it would. All it saw was a slightly fuzzy shield. There was no face, no sign of life. Worriedly he began to wonder if he had imagined the previous occasions. Perhaps they had been visions or dreams while he was sleeping, which on waking he had believed to have actually happened.

"Shield!" he whispered. "Do you have a message for me? Will you speak to me and tell me what I must do? Where is this goliard?"

He listened, but there was no voice speaking to him. There were only the sounds of activity in other parts of the inn: footsteps, muffled clatters – and a voice. But it was only a guest calling for water. Carlyon frowned, wondering if there was too much noise for him to hear the voice of the shield, but in the end he laid the shield back in its place next to his sword. As he prepared for bed, he glanced at it now and then, but nothing happened.

Nothing unexpected happened when he awoke the next morning, either. He washed and shaved and went downstairs for breakfast. While he ate, he discussed with James what they would do that day; where they would search. It was difficult to know what to do, and at the end of the meal it was with a heavy heart and a furrowed brow that Carlyon pushed himself up from the table. As he did so, he noticed a figure sitting in the inglenook nursing a pot of small beer. This surprised him, as he was sure that there had been no one there when he came into the room. He had stood by the fire to warm himself, before sitting at the table. He would have seen anyone in the inglenook. Nor could he understand how the man had slipped in during the meal without being noticed, for he had had a good view of the fireplace.

He looked closely across at the man and saw him lift his hand to beckon him over. It was almost as if the stranger had been waiting to catch his eye. In a few strides, Carlyon crossed the room. The man wordlessly indicated a nearby stool and Carlyon sat down to observe him. He saw an old man with long grey hair that was thinning on top. A straggly grey beard surrounded a mouth which had lost many of its teeth, but as Carlyon looked, he saw also that he was being closely observed by blue eyes that radiated kindness and experience. Carlyon shifted a little uncomfortably on the stool. The man was dressed like a peasant, and Carlyon wondered why he had felt the need to come and sit by him as if he was the inferior. He thought that he had better speak and then he could leave.

"I'm seeking a goliard," he said, putting authority into his words. "Do you know where I can find such a man?"

The stranger gave a gap-toothed smile and nodded. He put the hand holding his ale into his lap. Then he moved his head back slightly to look into Carlyon's eyes. "My name is Hal," he said, speaking clearly in the local accent. "I was told by Roderick Hoseford that you were seeking such a man. I'm a goliard. I've many a rhyme and many a story. Would you like me to tell you one? I've travelled all over the country and I've seen many wondrous things."

"I'm only interested in one story. I've heard tell of a place where, after a swan dies, flowers will grow in its place. Do you know that story?"

"The flowers of the swan? Yea, I've seen such a place, and much good it did me."

"You know where I can find such flowers? Tell me how to get there."

"So you seek the flowers of the swan?"

Hal's expression had changed from amused patronage of a possible customer to thoughtful contemplation. Carlyon saw that he was no longer looking at him, but was staring beyond him.

He seemed to be seeing through the walls of the inn into another world. Carlyon felt a shiver of fear trickle down his back, and he shifted again on his stool.

With a jerk, Hal's gaze fastened on him once more. "That's a difficult and dangerous search," he told him. "But I see you must undertake it. The love of a good woman is awaiting you. However, there are few who find the flowers, and fewer still who live to enjoy 'em."

"What do you mean?"

"There's a curse on whoever picks the flowers. It's a brave man, or a fool, who will seek to pick 'em."

"I have to pick them! Surely there is a way to avert the curse?" Carlyon leaned forward, as if worry were a weight on his back. He lifted his hand beseechingly. For an instant, it seemed that he was about to touch the old man.

Hal put his head on one side and contemplated him. Then he took a sip of his ale, while Carlyon waited impatiently. "You have to pick the flowers of the swan? Yea, I believe that to be so. The curse can be averted. Before picking, he who wishes to do so must first sprinkle the flowers with water that has been given him by a maiden who loves him."

"I'll do that! I'll do that! Where will I get such water?"

Hal sighed and said, "There are maidens to be found. But first you must know where to find the flowers."

"Yes, of course. Where will I find them?"

"There is one place I know of. You must go to the west and north, following the valley through which the River Trent flows. When this flow becomes a trickle, you must turn to the left and follow an ancient track, which will take you into the Wirral. In a forest there, you'll find a clearing with a pool. That's where I have seen a swan come to die."

"Will I be able to find this clearing? Is the forest large?"

"The forest is large enough, but worry you not. You'll find your way through it and the place you seek will be plain enough."

Not totally convinced, but lacking anything firmer, Carlyon nodded and thanked the wise old man for his help. After giving him some money, he got to his feet. He was feeling more confident now. Setting his jaw firmly, he turned to walk away from the fireside, but Hal spoke again.

"There's one more thing, young sir. You must be careful. There's evil abroad. I can sense you're being pursued. Leave quickly now and make all speed with your journey. Should anyone come here seeking, I'll try to delay them. Go! Wait no longer!"

Carlyon looked at the goliard with his eyes wide, unable to move at first. Then a tremor ran down his spine, as if an icy hand had touched him. He nodded and called abruptly to James to prepare for their departure.

They were soon on their way. A sleety rain was blowing across them, but it quickly blew itself out as they left Nottingham behind. After a few miles Carlyon looked back and saw the castle, standing stark against a lightening sky. He had been thinking about Patrina while he rode, hunched up in his saddle. He remembered that when he last left Nottingham, it had been in her company and in much brighter conditions. Then momentarily he wondered how the outlaw Rod and his band were faring, now that winter had come and they no longer had the shelter of the greenwood. He had never thought about that. Would they be safe in Nottingham?

He turned his head back and looked at the road ahead, as Champion clipped his way through the mud and the puddles. At least thinking about Patrina and the past had kept his mind occupied. It had helped to stop him from feeling too uncomfortable in the cold. Then sudden irritation made him jerk at the reins. It flashed into his mind that he had intended to go down to the river before leaving Nottingham. He had wanted to see if he could find any swans, so that he could feed them the corn, which he still had in his saddle pouch. He had been in such a haste to leave, and so busy with thoughts of Patrina, that his intention had completely slipped his mind. He shook his head and gritted his teeth. There was nothing that he could do now. He would watch out for swans as they followed the river and hope that in the meantime nothing unlucky happened to him. He would be bound to come across some. Looking up, he gazed at the shrouded horizon and hope filled his breast like a refreshing breath.

# 8

As Carlyon and James moved along the Trent Valley, the wind shifted. Overnight, it set into the south-west, bringing slightly warmer air. This would have made travel more pleasant, except that it brought rain with it. The roads were turned quickly into quagmires, through which their horses struggled slowly and exhaustingly. Days passed, as often they had to go many miles out of their way to get round the floodplain. Carlyon thought at times that there would never be an end, but gradually the river began to seem narrower, each time they glimpsed it from the highway.

Finally one day they reached a bleak, open place, where the river became little more than a brook. Breezes were fanning by fits the rustling sedge at the water's edge, and Carlyon reined in Champion. He pursed his lips to consider, thankful that the rain had no longer been following them that day. The clouds broke, and a shaft of sunlight illuminated a large rock some distance in front of them.

"Is that the way we have to go?" asked James.

"I'm not sure. We should be going off to the left, I ween, but I've seen no track for us to take. We'd best go on a little and see."

Carlyon was about to spur Champion into motion, when he saw a man come from behind the rock, herding a small flock of sheep. The wind had been blowing away the sound of the animals, but now that Carlyon could see them, he caught snatches of their bleating. He and James rode towards the flock, and when they met up, Carlyon hailed the shepherd.

"Greetings, good man! Can you tell me what place this is?"

"Biddulph Moor, sir."

"Is there a road from here going westwards over there?"

The shepherd looked to where Carlyon was pointing and then turned to indicate back along the track down which he had come. "There is such a one, sir. In the lee of yon rock, there's an ancient drover's road. Follow it towards Congleton. They say it goes all the way to Wales."

Leaving the man to regroup his flock, Carlyon and James pressed on. When they reached the rock, they turned left and followed a broad track towards the west. They stopped for the night at an inn, but when they awoke the next morning they found the whole town shrouded in fog. It was not impenetrable, though, and after they had got out into open country they found that visibility was a good ten yards or more. Their road could be clearly seen, and although the swirling fog brought on a sense of disorientation, Carlyon was confident that he would be able to find his way.

Occasionally a hamlet or a larger habitation would loom up before them; the evidence of life giving them a welcome reassurance. Fortunately their road was not too miry and they made good time. Towards midday they came upon an ale kitchen, where they were able to take their dinner, washed down with a spicy nut-brown brew.

When questioned about the fog, the alewife was sanguine. "It may have lifted by this even, sir. But it may be like to last for days. We let it do what it wills in these parts."

Nor was she much help when asked about the road to the Wirral.

"That'll be to the west. I've heard of that, but I've never travelled in that direction. I seldom go farther than the market in Knutsford. Mayhap at times I'll go slightly beyond to Macclesfield."

Later that afternoon, however, the fog began to lift and they had no trouble finding lodgings for the night. While unsaddling, Carlyon asked the ostler for the name of the place. He was taken aback when told that they were near to a village called Hulme. The name was not unfamiliar to Carlyon, but he had not expected to be there. If so, it meant that they had gone well out of their way. So he asked again, in order to confirm that it was not some other village of the same name. He could not understand how he had gone astray. Irritation at what had happened made him move jerkily. When James asked him if he was looking forward to a drink, he merely grunted in his preoccupation. This followed him into the inn, and it was not until he was actually sitting with a drink in front of him that he gave his attention to James. He told him that they had missed their way and seemed to have gone north rather than west.

"I know not how it happened. I was sure our road was going westwards."

"I also. I can't remember us turning northwards."

"It was so odd in the fog. I recall a fork not long after we left Congleton, but the left road went south, I'm sure of it. It was the right fork which led to the west."

"We must have been mistaken. Our road must have turned to the north so gently that we knew it not. So we were confused when we came to the fork."

"So be it. We could tell nothing in the fog. We could have gone in a circle, had evil spirits so wished it. We would have known nothing."

"What is this place we've come to?"

"It's very strange that we should have been led here. Perhaps it's fate. We're close to Hulme, which is where the Denneton family is from. The earl himself was born on the family estate there." Carlyon looked at James with a lighter face. He was beginning to think that they had been brought out of their way for a reason. Perhaps in some way Patrina was guiding him. Filled with hope, he finished off his drink and told James that they could not be too far from their journey's end. "By the day after the morrow we'll surely be in the Wirral Forest. There we shall find the flowers."

"And the task will be completed and we can go home again. I had been wondering how long we would have to wander."

"I also. But the end is in sight, God willing." Carlyon smiled his satisfaction. He had been anxious about how long his search would take. He had doubts about Patrina's steadfastness, for he suspected that patience was not a virtue which she held dear to her heart. John was a handsome and a doughty man. If Patrina was surrounded by temptation, Carlyon worried that she would not be strong enough to resist.

When he woke up the next morning, the fog had returned; thicker than ever, it seemed. He went out, but had walked no more than a dozen paces before he realised that it would be foolish to travel. Reluctantly, he went back into the inn for his breakfast. Afterwards, he spent an impatient morning praying for the fog to lift. As if in answer to his prayers, a breeze began to whisper round the building late in the morning, and by the time they had had their dinner, a weak December sun was shining low in the sky.

Carlyon lost no time in preparing for departure. Using the sun, he struck out off the highway, once they had gone a mile or so, to go a little south of west. He was hoping in that way to get back onto his correct route. This direction took them through woodland, which worried James. He spoke about the fog returning, or about robbers lying in wait. Carlyon calmed his superstitious fears and said that he was sure they would be safe. Even so, the wood was more extensive than he had expected.

He was beginning to wonder if they would be through it before nightfall, when they came upon a small cottage. Smoke was coming out through the hole in the roof, so, as it was late afternoon, he decided to seek hospitality there. While they were riding up to the door, a young woman came out and looked at them curiously. Carlyon estimated that she was about eighteen years old. She was not tall, and beneath her simple, undyed woollen robe, he saw that she had a chubby body. Her light brown hair was tied in two braids at either side of her well-shaped head, and two bright blue eyes shone out of a very pretty face, which was made the more interesting by a slightly crooked nose. He took all this in during the short time it took him to reach her door, and as he reined in, she gave him a welcoming smile that seemed to reach right into his heart. Coming to a halt, he rested his hands on his pommel and leaned forward to look down at her.

"Good day, fair maiden. We're travelling through here on our way to the Wirral. Can we rest here for the night?"

"Gladly, sirs. Your horses can be left there." She pointed to a small lean-to, in which there was an old wooden manger. "We've nought but a little hay—"

Carlyon raised a hand to interrupt her and said, "We have a sack of oats. A little hay will suffice."

He dismounted, flexed his legs a little, and handed the reins to James, who led the horses over to the lean-to. While James began to unsaddle them, Carlyon was introducing himself to the maiden.

"My name is Sir Carlyon de Bernedeslaw, and that is my squire, James Morton."

The young woman curtsied slightly and said, "I'm Mary, the thatcher's daughter. Please to come inside for a little refreshment."

She slipped neatly through the doorway and Carlyon followed her. In the gloom, he looked around. The cottage was as he'd expected. There was one bed against the far wall, with one or perhaps two spare straw mattresses underneath it. The other furniture consisted of a small trestle table, two benches, a chest and a cupboard. It would be crowded with everyone in there that night.

"Will your father be home soon?" he asked, eager to check whether he and James ought to travel on to seek other accommodation.

"My father's dead, sir."

Struck by the sudden shadow of sadness that darkened her face, he said, "I'm sorry to hear that. Do you live here on your own?"

"No, sir. This cottage belongs to a forester called Thomas. My home is some miles away near the River Mersey. Thomas took me away a few weeks ago. I have to keep house for him here. He says I must marry him. I think I must do it, although I don't want to."

While she had been speaking, she had been taking out two mugs and pouring in beer from a flagon. Now she turned and looked at Carlyon, and the helpless appeal in her blue eyes almost seared his face with its gentle beauty; a beauty he thought as fresh as April and as sweet as June. He could not understand why she should have to marry a man against her will. Then he remembered that she had told him that her father was dead.

"You have no relative to protect you? No uncle, no brother?"

"I have two brothers, but Thomas is a wizard. He has many potent spells and he's said he'll harm my brothers and my sister if I don't stay with him."

Carlyon felt a tremor at her sad words. Despite the small fire in the centre of the room, he suddenly felt cold, and he put his hand to the dagger on his belt for reassurance. There was something about the cottage which worried him. It was as if there was a bad presence hovering like the smoke from the fire. A noise at his back startled him and he jerked round, but it was only James coming in. Carlyon tried to cover his nervousness by pointlessly asking him if he had settled the horses. As James was answering, Mary stepped forward with the two mugs of ale and Carlyon felt a calm sweetness come from her like the scent of violets. He smiled and took a mug.

"Thank you, my dear. I wish you well."

As he drank, he saw a look of concern on her face. She was watching James, and Carlyon also glanced at him. His squire had grimaced when he lifted his mug to his mouth, and now he passed the mug into his other hand.

"Do you have some injury, sir?" Mary asked sympathetically.

"It's nought. I knocked my arm on the branch of a tree while riding, and I think I strained it more while settling the horses."

"Perhaps I can do something. Uncover your arm." She turned and went to the chest, from which she took a small piece of linen. Dipping it into a pan of hot water simmering on the fire, she wrung it out and went to a small pot by the cupboard. From that she took a herb, which she crushed between her fingers. After folding the cloth into a pad, she spread the crushed herb over it. "Give me your arm, sir."

James turned towards her and she placed the hot compress on the bruise. Tenderly, she then bound it with another strip of cloth. Carlyon watched all this with pleased interest, impressed by the capable way in which Mary was dealing with the matter. He almost wished that he too had a slight injury, so that he could call on her kindliness and compassion.

"Who is this man Thomas?" he asked, suddenly wanting to help her. "How did he get you here?"

"I was on my way to visit my brother, who lives a few miles to the west. Thomas saw me in the wood and told me he wanted me. He showed me his power and said he would harm my brother and his family if I didn't go with him. He's kept me in this cottage ever since and nobody knows I'm here."

"It's not right for you to be held here away from your family. I'll wait until this Thomas comes back and I'll tell him I'm taking you away with me. If he refuses or threatens harm to your family, then I'll kill him."

"Oh, sir, please don't do anything rash. Thomas is protected by powerful magic. It won't be easy to kill him. He may harm you. Perhaps it would be better if you left. I fear for you."

Carlyon drew in a breath and smiled reassuringly at Mary. She was standing before him, both hands clenched together. Despite the worried pleading in her eyes, he could sense the hope which was blowing in her breast. Her beauty almost overthrew him, and he vowed to himself that he would do all he could to rescue her. "It's too late for us to travel on now. We won't find anywhere else to rest for the night. You carry on with your business. I see you're preparing a meal. We'll wait here for Thomas."

He went over and sat on one of the benches, leaning his back against the edge of the table, so that he could face into the room. At his signal James came to join him, wrapping his gawky frame over the bench, but Mary still stood where she was, looking anxiously at her would-be rescuer. Carlyon smiled, nodded, and made an encouraging gesture with his hand, so she let out her breath and went to the fire. The two men watched as she added turnip, chopped leek and artichokes to the boiling water in the pan. Then she went out to milk the cow.

While she was gone, James screwed up his face in thought. Then he turned to Carlyon and asked, "Should we be stopping here, sire? You have a task to complete. Should you be risking yourself in this dangerous place? I'm fearful."

"I know I've got an important task, James. I'm determined to complete it. But I'm sure I've been brought here for a purpose. There's something I've got to do here. It's a strange place, but I feel that this maiden must be protected."

James did not seem reassured, but he had no choice except to trust his master. Carlyon looked at him, knowing that not only Mary, but also his squire was relying on him for protection. He hoped that he was doing the right thing.

Thomas returned home just after sunset. When he entered the cottage, Carlyon noticed that he did not seem surprised to find two strangers there. Carlyon's first thought was that it was almost as if he had been expecting them, but then he realised that Thomas would have seen the horses hobbled outside the cottage. Thomas walked to the fire and put down his bag. Without greeting the strangers in his home, he put out his grimy hands to warm them at the flames. This gave Carlyon a chance to observe him closely and try to get his measure. He saw an old man – perhaps over fifty years of age; certainly not far off. His greying hair was thin and he had a narrow face. His long chin was covered by a short but straggly beard. He was not so tall as Carlyon and not so well built, although he was wiry. Carlyon judged that in physical combat he would be able to best Thomas with ease. If it came to that.

As if he had been deliberately taking his time, Thomas then took the mug of warm milk infused with cinnamon which Mary had been holding ready for him. Carlyon could not fail to note how submissive she seemed. He gritted his teeth, unable to understand why he was angry at that. Thomas took a sip of his drink and finally turned to look at his guests.

"Good even, gentlemen," he said, smiling insolently. "I seldom see strangers here. What brings you past my door?"

"Good even, Thomas," said Carlyon, who stayed seated and was gratified on seeing Thomas's eyes widen at the use of his name. However, he hurried on when he caught the furious glance which Thomas threw at Mary. "I'm Sir Carlyon de Bernedeslaw. I and my squire are on our way to the Wirral and we've been overtaken by the night."

"This is not the way to the Wirral. The high road is south of here. How have you come through this wood to my house?"

Thomas looked at Carlyon with eyes narrowed by cold suspicion. Carlyon stayed calm, lolling nonchalantly back against the table. He felt that he now had the measure of the man.

"We lost our way in yesterday's fog on leaving Congleton. I thought it would be more direct, and save time, if we cut through this wood. Perhaps we were lucky to find your cottage, or we would have been benighted on the road."

"It may be more direct, if one knows the way through the forest, but it's easy to go astray here. Stay the night with me, sirs, and I'll put you on the right way tomorrow morn."

This fellow seems very sure of himself, thought Carlyon grimly. He's almost arrogant. He seems to think he's my equal. He thanked Thomas for his offer of hospitality and patronisingly nodded his head in acknowledgement.

Thomas wasted no time. He turned and spoke to Mary, the sharpness of his tone ringing round the room like steel. "Serve out food for our guests, Mary! I'm ready to eat now."

Mary moved quickly and submissively. She found two extra bowls and served out the stew which she had made. She carried the first bowl over to Carlyon. He had been lounging on the bench with his legs stretched out in front of him ever since Thomas had entered the cottage. He now jumped alertly to his feet; partly out of politeness, but mainly so that he could turn and sit at the table. James did the same and was served next. Then Thomas, who had taken a place at the table opposite James. Finally Mary served herself, but not before she had brought out some bread that she had baked that morning. When all the men had been given food, she meekly came to sit opposite Carlyon. As she did so, she glanced knowingly at him from beneath her lashes and he sensed a hint of iron behind her air of humility. He kept his face impassive, but he glanced at Thomas, who had placed both his hands on his bowl, ready to lift it.

Before reaching for his bowl, Carlyon told himself that he would need to be watchful and careful while they were in the cottage. Glancing at Mary, who was looking down at her bowl, he lifted his own and took a sip. It was still too hot, so he reached for some bread to dip into it. While he was doing this, he moved his legs under the narrow table and his stockinged feet accidentally touched Mary's feet. He felt the coldness of her bare skin and, as she did not move, gently rested his feet upon hers to warm them. She gave no sign of recognition. Her head stayed bent, but Carlyon knew that she was thanking him. His pleasant musing was interrupted by Thomas. He had been looking sideways at Carlyon, and he asked what his business was in the Wirral.

"I'm seeking a place where swans go to die. I've heard tell of such a place in that part of the world. Do you know of it?"

Thomas shook his head and said that he knew nothing about swans, although he had heard that the Wirral was a wild place where strange things happened. He asked why Carlyon was interested in where swans died, and Carlyon told him about the legend, and that he wanted to take some of the flowers. Thomas nodded carelessly. He speared a piece of salted pork from his bowl with his knife and put it in his mouth without further comment. Carlyon continued to eat, as it helped to take his mind off what he knew he would have to say before long. Thomas, in his untidy tunic, looked like a peasant, and yet there was something about him which worried Carlyon. There was a sense of self-assurance that belied his class. There was an aura of menace about him, a brooding presence, as if he had access to unseen power. Carlyon was particularly struck by the way in which Thomas frequently looked sideways at him, with his eyes half closed, yet everywhere. He seemed to suspect him of something. If Carlyon, a man, was made nervous by Thomas, he could understand how Mary would be frightened of what he might do. They finished off their meal in what Carlyon felt was an uneasy silence, but when Mary got up to pour out some more ale, Thomas spoke.

"I'll take you with me tomorrow morn, to show you your way out of the forest and put you on your road. It's not far, but it's easy to get lost."

"Good. I thank you for that," said Carlyon, and then, almost without drawing breath, he went on. "I'll be taking Mary with me. She has to go back to her family and I don't want them to be harmed. I'm taking them under my protection."

He tensed and held himself ready for anything. He truly believed that anything could happen. Mary had stopped what she was doing. She stood still, a mug of poured ale in her hand, as if not wanting to draw attention to herself. She was looking fearfully at Thomas, but when Carlyon glanced at her, he saw in her face also a hope that she was about to be freed. This strengthened his nerves, knowing that she was relying on him, and he looked back at Thomas with renewed determination. He knew that he was not alone. He had felt James at his side become tense and watchful, ready to support him. Momentarily, he wondered if James was as fearful as he was that Thomas might use some magic to overpower them.

The silence that had fallen since Carlyon had declared his intention continued. Thomas's face had set grimly at his words, but then it relaxed almost immediately. It was as if he knew something which the others did not. He leaned back against the wall and put both his hands on the table. This made Carlyon think that he was about to leap over it at him. He looked quickly to the side where his sword stood propped against the wall with his shield. It was within reach and the firelight flickered on its hilt, making it seem alive. It was calling to him, and he was prepared.

# 9

The gloom in the cottage was relieved only by the fire and one small rushlight. Carlyon was sitting with his back to the fire and could see Thomas's face clearly. He watched carefully, and as he did so, he saw a smile start to curl the corners of the old man's thin lips. The sight did not make him relax, because he sensed it to be a smile of impertinent arrogance. Anger tightened Carlyon's mouth at the thought that Thomas was still so sure of himself. He had no right to be so calm. Carlyon took a breath, and was thinking of saying that they would leave immediately, darkness or not, when Thomas at last spoke.

"So, Sir Knight, you've seen my little treasure and you want her for yourself?"

The patronising sneer of his voice was like a slap to Carlyon's ear. He thrust a vehement authority into his answer and spoke more loudly than he'd intended.

"That's certainly not the case. I simply want to restore her to her family."

He glanced at Mary, intending to encourage her, but he thought he saw a shadow of disappointment flit across her face. Perhaps he had spoken more forcefully than was necessary?

However, he had no time to reflect on it, because Thomas had taken his hands from the table and folded them in front of his chest.

"I see we have a truly perfect gentle knight," Thomas scoffed. "You are rescuing this poor damsel out of purity."

"I'm rescuing her because it's the right thing to do."

"So you say. But Mary is not free to be rescued. She belongs to me and I'll keep her."

"If I have to fight for her, I will. I'll defeat whatever you call up against me."

"Brave words, Sir Knight, and I'm impressed. You amuse me, thinking that you're stronger than me. No matter. It's a long time since I was amused, and I'm minded to have a little fun at your expense."

Carlyon tensed, wondering what was about to come, but Thomas merely unfolded his arms and thoughtfully stroked his beard with his left hand.

"I won't give you a straight refusal," he said sinisterly. "I'll set you three simple tasks. If you complete them, I'll give you my word that you can leave safely with your damsel. Do you agree?"

"What are these tasks?"

"Simple, I assure you. You can carry them out here. I'll tell you them tomorrow. Do you agree?"

Realising that he had no choice, Carlyon said that he agreed, and Thomas nodded his satisfaction. He told Mary sharply to bring the ale, and then insolently raised his glass for a toast.

"Here's to the morrow."

Carlyon did not join him, but he drank his ale and thoughtfully watched Thomas, who was behaving as though everything was normal. There was nothing that Carlyon could do but wait on him. This was a delay that he had not foreseen. Already the search for the flowers was taking longer than he had expected. Lady Patrina would be waiting impatiently. Sir John also would not be sitting on his hands. God willing, Thomas's tasks would be quickly completed.

When Mary went out to bring in the cow, their few hens having been brought in before it was dark, Carlyon sent James out to check on the horses. He then took the opportunity to ask Thomas if he had decided what the tasks would be.

"You'll learn that tomorrow morn," Thomas told him loftily, seeming to enjoy keeping him in suspense.

Carlyon was not prepared to cajole or beg. He also knew that any threat of force would serve no purpose, so he turned his back on Thomas. When Mary came in again, he went outside to the privy. On his return he saw that she and Thomas had already hung a large cloth across the room to divide out the sleeping chamber. Thomas gave up the bed to the two guests, while he and Mary slept on mattresses on the floor.

It was not a very comfortable night, and it was still dark when Carlyon awoke. He stayed in the bed until glimmers of light appeared and he heard Mary turning out the animals and striking a flint for the fire. Pulling himself upright, he climbed off the bed and put on his overclothes. Moving aside the curtain slightly, he bent and passed through. Mary smiled sweetly and, in a soft voice that floated into his heart, wished him a good morning. He greeted her equally softly; almost as if they had met in a secret tryst. She handed him a bowl and a piece of soap, and he went out to the well to wash his hands and face. While he was drying himself, Mary too came out to wash. Without thinking, he poured out his water and put some fresh in the bowl for her. While she bent over the bowl, he stamped slightly and remarked that it seemed that they would have a fine day. He was making conversation, because he wanted to stay with her and watch her gentle movements as she washed her face.

They were interrupted in their brief idyll by Thomas coming out of the cottage, closely followed by James. Carlyon ignored the mock humility in Thomas's greeting, and answered him civilly before taking up the pail of water to carry it into the cottage for Mary. Thomas did not seem to mind that the two of them had been alone for a few minutes, but Mary immediately busied herself with cleaning the floor. Carlyon sat on a bench to watch her, and to wonder what lay in store for him after his hasty promise to rescue her.

He was kept waiting. After a simple breakfast of bread and ale, Thomas sat for a while, honing his knife. At last he got to his feet.

"Come along, Sir Knight, and I'll show you what I want you to do."

He went to a corner of the room and Carlyon saw there three bushel measures. Each one was filled with barley. Thomas picked up one and told Carlyon and James to take one each of the other two. Without further explanation he went outside, and so the others followed. In front of the cottage, Thomas put his pot on the ground and then looked around, as if estimating. Seemingly satisfied, he told the others to wait, and picked up his pot again. While they watched, he walked to and fro, emptying out the barley. He did the same with the other two pots, so that by the end a considerable area had been seeded.

"There you are, Sir Knight," he said triumphantly. "I'm going about my business now. While I'm away, I want you to pick up every grain by the time I return for dinner. That will be your first task." He smiled arrogantly and went into the cottage to collect his bag. When he came out, he told Mary to make extra bread for that evening. Barely glancing at Carlyon, he confidently bade him farewell, then disappeared amongst the trees.

Carlyon stepped over to look at his task. The grains of barley were easy to spot. As he peered more closely, however, he could see that many were hidden in the grass. It looked a hopeless task.

"We'll help, sire," said James at his shoulder. "With three of us, I'm sure we'll manage it."

"Of course we will." Mary sounded just as positive. "Let's make a start."

She immediately bent over to begin gathering some into a small pile. The other two joined her, and they worked industriously for some minutes. However, despite the nimbleness of Mary's fingers, the work progressed slowly and Carlyon began to lose heart. Then he had an idea. He remembered seeing Mary using a broom. He went into the cottage to look. It was leaning against the wall next to his shield. As he put his hand on the broom, he heard the low, sonorous voice of the shield speak to him.

"Look on top of the cupboard. There is a small box. Inside is a whistle which belongs to Thomas. Take the whistle outside, blow it three times, and then come into the cottage to wait. When you have finished, be sure to put the box back exactly as you found it."

Carlyon, who had turned his head to look at the cupboard, now looked back at the shield. Had it spoken? It was as it usually was. Gingerly, he reached out a hand to touch it with his fingertips. It was only metal. He thought to question the shield. Whose was the voice? Why was it speaking to him? But there was no time for that. He straightened up and hurried over to reach up to the top of the cupboard. Sure enough, there was a box. It was of rough unplaned wood. Inside it was a short and very ordinary-looking wooden whistle. Carlyon took it out and put it to his lips. Then, taking it from his mouth, he went outside. The others had not progressed much farther, but he called for their attention.

"Look! I've got Thomas's whistle. It has magic powers, I trow. I'll try it." He put it to his mouth and gave three good blasts. It was a high-pitched, not unpleasant sound, and it seemed to carry. Lowering the whistle, he looked carefully around at the scattered barley, but nothing happened. It was all unchanged. "We'd better go into the cottage," he said, and ushered the others in front of him.

Inside the cottage, they stood by the doorway and watched anxiously. Still nothing happened. Then the ground seemed to turn black, and they saw movement, as if it were rippling.

"See!" whispered James. "It's magic."

"No – look closely," said Mary after a few seconds. "It's a flock of starlings. They've come out of their roost."

"See now," whispered Carlyon. "Will they collect all the corn for us?"

Breathlessly, they watched. Carlyon looked down at the whistle cupped in his hand and was suddenly worried at this evidence of the power Thomas possessed. He wondered what the next two tasks would be, even if the first one were completed to Thomas's satisfaction.

The birds continued to peck, quickly and greedily. At last, one by one they began to fly up into the nearby trees and a satisfied squawking filled the air, covering the three humans with the sound.

"Thank you, birds," Mary said softly, and Carlyon repeated the sentiment himself.

He put the whistle carefully back in its box and then replaced it on top of the cupboard. Turning to the others, he said, with more optimism than he felt, that he hoped that the next two tasks would be as simple for him to complete. Mary and James added their prayers to that. Then Mary clapped her hands and said that she had bread to bake.

After midday, while they were waiting for Thomas to come home, nervousness began to settle over them like a mist creeping out from amongst the leafless trees. For the rest of the morning Mary and James kept themselves busy: Mary about her household work and James chopping firewood or seeing to their horses. Carlyon wandered about the area, wanting to fix the lie of the land in his mind, in case they had to make a hasty departure. Then he sat in the cottage with nothing to do but let his thoughts run as they would. At first he was confident that whatever Thomas proposed, he would be able to counter it; sure that he had good powers on his side. When Mary and James came to sit with him, it was then, with nothing to occupy her hands and mind, that Mary began to feel fearful.

"Thomas will be angry that the task was completed," she hazarded. "He'll wonder how we did it."

"I expect he'll realise that you two helped me, even though I was set the task. He'll only set a more difficult task next."

"I hope he'll keep his word."

"Can he be trusted?" mused James. "We saw some strange magic this morning. I'll warrant he has some other powers that he can use against us."

"He does," agreed Mary, "and I don't want to trust him. We must keep on our guard."

"I think we'll be safe until the tests have been completed," Carlyon told them, anxious to keep everyone's spirits up, including his own. "I have me the feeling that Thomas wishes to play with us. He'll want to finish it. We'll play along and stay watchful."

When Thomas came home, he was surprised when Carlyon pointed to where the barley had been strewn. He looked at Carlyon thoughtfully and then let his bag fall to the ground. Carlyon watched anxiously as Thomas searched the area, but at last he seemed satisfied. At least, Carlyon saw him straighten his back and return to the cottage.

Thomas looked sourly at Carlyon. "So, Sir Knight," he said, "you've completed that task. I'll set you your second on the morrow." He pushed past Carlyon with a grim face and called harshly to Mary to give him his warm milk.

Carlyon let out a sigh of relief and looked at the trees surrounding him. There was no sign of any birds; nor of anything other than a darkening December day. He hurried off to the privy at the side of the cottage, propelled by a sudden anxious urge.

The second night and the following dawn passed much as the first. The breakfast was the same, and after it, Thomas sat in thought, closely observed by Carlyon. Then he glanced sideways at Carlyon, his eyes narrowed. All at once, he got to his feet, picked up his bag and went outside. Carlyon was momentarily taken by surprise. He had expected Thomas to call him. For some seconds he continued to sit, thinking that Thomas would return. Nervously he squeezed his nostrils between his thumb and forefinger and then rubbed the finger down the tip of his nose. Suddenly it came to him that Thomas was wanting to catch him out. He jumped to his feet and ran outside. At first there was no sign of Thomas, but as he moved away from the cottage, he saw his quarry along the path. He was standing, and seeming to be contemplating a large fir tree. Carlyon walked up to him.

"So, you've come, Sir Knight. I thought me you'd given up and had no wish to do the second test."

"Not at all. I'm ready and willing. What is the test?"

"Here it is." And Thomas pointed to the fir tree.

"What of it? It's a tree. Tell me what I must do."

"Quietly, Sir Knight. There's no need for anger. It's a simple task. I want you to take every needle off that tree, and do it before I come home this afternoon."

Thomas laughed and set off down the path. Carlyon watched the confident swagger of his back, but smiled in satisfaction. It was not a difficult task; simply a time-consuming one. He turned and saw that Mary and James had come to join him. They asked about the task, and when he told them they shook their heads, but immediately made a start on the lower branches.

Carlyon decided to waste no time. Telling them that he would soon be back, he dashed into the cottage. Alone there, he stood in front of the shield and asked it what he should do. To his surprise, nothing happened. The shield stayed just as it was and gave no indication that it had ever had a face or a voice. Carlyon asked again for advice, but again there was nothing. Nonplussed, he scratched his chin, almost wondering again if it had all been his imagination. There was nothing for it. He would have to take the whistle again and see what happened when he blew it. He stepped over to the cupboard, but when he reached onto the top, his fingers found empty space. Anxiously he went and dragged a bench over and climbed up so that he could see the top. There was nothing there. Thomas had taken the whistle. Had he suspected? Then

Carlyon remembered that he had been told to put the whistle back exactly as he had found it. In his exuberance at completing the task, he had forgotten about that. Thomas must have noticed that the whistle had been moved. Carlyon sat on the bench and despair pushed his shoulders forward. He had seen the tree. He knew that even with three of them, the task would be difficult to do in the time. It was foolish to try. Perhaps he should give up? What else could he do?

Suddenly, the shield's voice jerked his head back, as if an icy shower had hit his face. "This is no time to be thinking of giving up. Mary is worth fighting for. You should never lose heart."

Carlyon got to his feet. Of course. He must fight. He listened as the voice rolled on.

"There is a pot of honey in the cupboard. Take it and mix it with warm water. Carry it carefully to the tree and climb to the top. As you climb down, sprinkle the mixture on the needles. When you reach the bottom, walk seven paces to a mound, which you will see near the tree. Strike this mound three times with the flat of your sword and then go back into the cottage."

Carlyon thanked the shield and quickly got up from the bench. He opened the cupboard and found the honey. There was a pan of water on the fire, so he used his knife to put in as much of the honey as he could scrape out. Hurriedly, but trying not to spill, he went out to the others. They were making slow progress, but he told them to step aside; he was going to try something. He then began to climb the tree, ascending with difficulty as he held on to the pan. Near the top he remembered that he had forgotten to bring his sword, but he shouted down to James, who ran off to get it for him. It was not an easy task to sprinkle the honeyed water on the needles, especially when he got lower down and the branches were larger, but, using a ladle, he did the best he could. Back on the ground, he turned from the tree and smiled at the other two, who were looking at him with a mixture of curiosity and hope. Putting the pan down by Mary's feet, he took his sword from James and looked about him. There was a mound just beyond the tree. It was not very high, but there seemed to be no other, and when Carlyon measured the distance, it was seven paces away. Not wanting to make a mistake, he checked again to assure himself that there was no other mound. Then he struck it smartly three times with the flat of his sword. He stood back, but nothing happened. Blowing out his breath sharply, he told the others to come to the cottage.

Anxiously they peered out through the doorway, but for a few minutes there seemed to be no change. Then, almost at the same time, all three saw a strange sight. The sun was slightly over to the left of the tree and not high in the sky. As a result, it was shining directly onto the tree, and as Carlyon and the others watched, they saw that the tree was shimmering in the sunlight, while seeming to be shedding its needles.

"It's magic!" whispered James, awe making his voice hoarse. "It's magic again."

"No, I think not," said Mary. "Can you see? They're wood ants coming from their nest in that mound. It's the honey. They're taking away the needles."

Now that there was an explanation, it did not seem quite so wondrous. Even so, the three of them continued to watch in amazement as the tree was stripped. When all was still, they went to look. Ants could yet be seen on the tree and not all of the needles had been removed, but it did not take long for Carlyon and James to climb the tree and finish off the job. The rest of the day was spent cheerfully. This time Carlyon had no worries about

Thomas's return. He was confident that he was more than a match for him. He suspected that after he had (perhaps unexpectedly) completed two tasks, Thomas would have a much more difficult one for the third day. However, Carlyon's confidence was such that he vowed to himself that, succeed or fail in that task, he would nevertheless take Mary with him when he left.

Thomas came home shortly before sunset. Carlyon was outside the cottage with James, watching as the latter groomed the horses in expectation of their departure the next day, and he saw Thomas stop at the denuded fir tree. He walked all the way round it twice, looked up into it, looked around, and even kicked the trunk, as if he could not believe his eyes. He then stalked to the cottage and, ignoring Carlyon, went inside. Throwing down his bag, he called harshly to Mary for his warm milk. Carlyon had followed him in, and now leaned against the doorpost. His arms were folded and he looked sardonically at the clearly irritated Thomas.

"I know not how you did it," snapped Thomas at last without looking at him. "But you've completed it and that's all there is to say. You've one final task. I'll set that on the morrow and I'll warrant you won't find it so easy. And I shall be with you this time, to watch."

It was an uncomfortable evening. Nobody was in any mood for conversation. Carlyon noticed how Mary's nervousness made her clumsy at times, and he was forced to intervene on one occasion, when Thomas reprimanded her. Thomas sneered and said that he would treat his chattel as he wished. She did not yet belong to Carlyon. However, he seemed to calm down, and if he had occasion to speak to Mary again, he spoke civilly, if with authority. Carlyon remained on his guard, but he was glad when preparations began to be made for retiring. Then, as he sat on the edge of the bed, he suddenly began to feel an overwhelming urge to sleep. He struggled to keep his eyelids open, and realised that somehow he had been drugged. His last sight, before his eyes closed and he fell back on the bed, was of James already asleep beside him and Mary curled up on a mattress, while Thomas stood and watched them all with a satisfied smile on his face.

Carlyon remembered nothing of the night. No dreams. No sounds. When he awoke, dawn streaked the sky, but it was still gloomy in the cottage, even with the light from the fireplace. He pulled himself upright and looked around. James was still sleeping, and Thomas was heating something in a pan on the fire. There was no sign of Mary.

"Where's Mary?" Carlyon called out angrily. "If you've harmed her, you'll pay for it."

He got to his feet and stepped forward threateningly, but Thomas raised a hand placatingly.

"Calm down, Sir Knight, calm down. Mary is quite safe. She's not here, but that's all part of your final task."

"You knave. You gave us a sleeping draught last night. If this is trickery, I'll have your black heart."

"Anger will serve you none. I had to make you sleep so that I could prepare everything. Come now, here's water. Wash yourself and I'll tell you what you must do."

Carlyon looked suspiciously at the bowl on the table, but without wasting more words, he shook James awake. Then he went and washed his hands and face. Feeling refreshed, he looked grimly at Thomas. "Tell me now. Where's Mary and what must I do to free her from your tyranny?"

"Such haste, Sir Knight. Well, mayhap it should be done quickly and then you can be on your way. Come with me."

Carlyon followed him out of the cottage, ready for a trick, but unable to do anything else. Outside, there was plenty of light, although the sun was hidden yet by a bank of cloud. There was no breeze, but the air was cold. Frequent and thick, chilly beads of frost gemmed the crispy blades of grass. On the bare ground in front of the cottage, Carlyon saw three blankets which were covering three upright figures, each one about five and a half feet tall.

"There you are," said Thomas gleefully, indicating them.

"What's this? Are they statues to unveil?"

"Ha, ha, ha! You are right. Two of them are tree trunks. One of them is Mary. But which one? You have one chance to choose. If you choose wrongly, then she stays with me. Make you your choice."

Carlyon stood and looked. Nervously, he licked his lips. Each blanket seemed exactly the same. Each shape seemed exactly the same. There seemed nothing to choose between them...except that, from a certain angle, the one on the right had slight curves to it, as if the blanket were covering a human body. There was just sufficient difference to draw his attention. A noise behind him made him look round. It was only James coming out of the cottage, his face reflecting the anxiety that was on Carlyon's.

"Hurry now, Sir Knight. Make your choice," said Thomas.

His confidence made Carlyon pause. Doubt gripped him by the throat, but he knew that he would have to choose and live with the decision – for better or worse. Nervously, he pinched his nostrils with his thumb and forefinger. Then, as he was about to move, the sun slipped out above the cloud. A shaft of sunlight came through the trees to illuminate the three blankets. Abruptly Carlyon said, "I choose the one on the left." Before Thomas could say or do anything, he marched over and began to pull off the blanket.

# 10

*T*he gasp which James gave was the only sound at first. Carlyon was too relieved to say anything. He was sure, when he moved, that he had chosen the correct blanket. Even so, at the back of his mind there was a fear that Thomas might have done something to trick him. It was only when the blanket began to reveal its secret that he relaxed and felt faint relief flood his body, as if it were flowing out of the blanket and through his arm.

The blanket was covering a light wooden framework, which gave it the shape of a tree trunk. Inside the frame was a post, and as Carlyon pulled the blanket, he saw first Mary's feet, then her dress, and finally her head. He smiled triumphantly and let the blanket fall unheeded from his hand. The relief in Mary's eyes pulled at his heart like joyful cords and her discovered beauty almost made him sway. Drawing in his breath sharply, he reached forward and untied the gag from her mouth. As she gasped and thanked him, he took his dagger and cut her loose from the post. The bonds fell away and he held her when she staggered forward. Holding her protectively, he turned to Thomas.

"There you are! I've carried out all three tasks correctly. Mary is no longer in your power. I'll take her away with me, and I vow by all the saints that if you do any harm to her or her family, I'll hunt you down."

"There's no need for that, Sir Knight." Thomas's tone was surly and his fury brought flecks of foam into the corners of his mouth. His hands were clenched angrily and Carlyon held himself tensed, but Thomas made no threatening move. "I know not how you managed to complete the tasks," he went on immediately. "You have some power that's greater than mine. So be it – this time. I've given my word and I'll keep it. You may take away your prize, and may she serve you well."

Thomas sighed and Carlyon saw his fists unclench. He thought he detected sadness in Thomas's face. He could believe that she was a woman that any man could love. However, she did not want to marry Thomas and she should not have to marry against her will, unless her liege lord decreed otherwise.

Thomas was looking sideways at him, as if considering something. Then he jerked his head up and spoke. "You must leave now, but first break your fast with me."

He smiled and indicated the open door of the cottage, but Carlyon felt Mary's body stiffen beneath the arm which he still had round her. He suspected a trick on Thomas's part, remembering the previous night's sleeping potion, so he shook his head.

"We can't do that," he said flatly. "We must be on our way. I've stayed here longer than I expected and I want to be at the Wirral by Christmas."

Thomas's body slumped slightly in disappointment, but he stood aside as Carlyon and Mary went into the cottage to collect the bags. Mary's possessions were few: only a knife and a small casket. Carlyon put them in his bag, which he carried out with James's. Outside, James was finishing off the saddling of the horses, watched by a silent Thomas. Carlyon glanced warily at him, but said nothing as he handed the bags to James to be loaded onto the packhorse. He took out a spare travelling cloak for Mary, which she put over her head and shoulders. When he climbed up on Champion, he pulled her up behind him. She put her arms round him and they were ready to leave.

Thomas seemed to shake himself. He pulled his weather-soiled hood over his thin hair and stepped forward. "I'll see you on your way. It's best that you don't go astray." He lowered his eyes and walked off through the trees.

Carlyon hesitated, but then kicked Champion into motion. Without speaking, he and James followed their guide.

Thomas led them for about a hundred yards or so, and at last came out onto a recognisable, if narrow, pathway. He stood to one side and pointed. "If you follow that, it'll bring you to the highway which will take you to the Wirral. There you'll find what you seek."

Carlyon nodded, relieved that they were getting away without the need for violence. The three horses filed slowly past Thomas, who watched for some seconds before turning to go back to his cottage. Carlyon and his party did not look back, and they had not travelled far when James spoke.

"Can you tell me, sire, how you made the right choice? All the blankets looked the same to me, except that I thought the one on the right had a woman's form beneath it."

"Yes," said Mary brightly, "I also would like to know that."

"It proved to be simple. The one on the right did indeed appear to conceal a slight woman's form, but that was a trick of

Thomas's. I knew not what to do and I didn't want to fail. I was about to choose the one on the right, and praying it would be Mary, when the sun came out of the cloud and shone on the three blankets. Then I saw plainly. Only two of the blankets had frost on them, and so the third one must have been put there just before dawn. I knew that that was Mary."

He felt her arms tighten round him in a brief, delighted hug, and was unexpectedly pleased by it. When they'd first set off from Thomas's cottage, he had wished that they had a saddle on the packhorse. However, as they had travelled through the trees, the warmth of her body against his back had become very pleasant and comfortable, and he was now happy for it to continue.

Cheerfully, the three of them continued for half an hour or so, until at last Carlyon could see that the trees were thinning out. It was with relief that he led them out of the wood and saw the main highway, as Thomas had said. Carlyon reined in, and felt Mary jerk. He smiled, because he had felt her head on his shoulder and he knew that she had been drowsing. It made him feel protective, and so he had done nothing to disturb her. Now he apologised.

"I'm sorry to awaken you, Mary, but we've reached the highway now."

"No, sir, I shouldn't sleep, but I had a restless night."

She had moved away from him, embarrassed by her familiarity, and disappointment sent a cold breath down Carlyon's back when he felt her arms loosen their grip. He covered with his gloved hand one of her hands, which was resting lightly on his waist, and pressed it slightly in reassurance.

"I pray you're rested. I fear we still have a long way to travel." Then he pointed down the road to his right and addressed James.

"That way lies the Wirral and our journey's end. If we follow it awhile, we can turn off and go to Mary's brother's house." He paused. Mary could not be left by the side of the road. His duty would not be completed until he delivered her safely, but he knew that such a detour would delay them even more. It would give the witch time to catch up with them. He looked to his left. "I want to go that way. The witch is behind us. I'll warrant that Thomas will show her where we've gone. If we go this way, we can go round this forest and then go down to the Wirral from the north. If the witch follows Thomas's directions, she'll go awrong, and when she discovers our new road, we'll be well in front of her." Then, to Mary, "This will cause a delay before I can take you to your brother's home. Will you travel with us, or do you wish to make your way from here?"

"I'll travel with you, sir, if I may. I'll feel safer."

Carlyon noticed that she had answered immediately; almost as if she had not had to consider it. The muscles of his face moved in comfortable pleasure to know that he would have her company for a little while yet. He lifted his head and looked keenly down the road. "So be it. We three shall travel together. Let's be on our way. I doubt we'll have to go far before we find a place where we can take some refreshment. Then we must make haste. Christmas is nigh and I fear we'll still be on the road. I don't know how merry we'll be."

Lady Patrina Denneton was expecting her Christmas to be a merry affair. Preparations in her father's house began early, and by the time Christmas Eve was upon them the store cupboards in the kitchen were filled with all that would be necessary for the twelve days of the festivities. In the morning of Christmas Eve, the bailiff sent out two men to gather streamers of ivy and boughs of green fir, which were taken in to decorate the great hall. The chamberlain checked that all of his staff were sure of their duties and that they had everything they required. The steward ordered a man to shovel out the privies, and ensured that there were some extra-large logs for the fires. The days were dark and cold, but Lady Patrina knew that here in her father's home, her days would be warm and bright. She knew that she would be given much amusement. Eagerly, she waited for it all to begin.

First thing on Christmas morning, the whole household crowded into the small chapel with the earl and his family, while the chaplain led them in prayers. Then, when at last the Christmas service came to an end, Patrina was pleased to find that John had contrived to walk next to her as she followed her father out. She glanced at him, but then modestly bowed her head, suddenly driven to tease him. To her disappointment, he seemed to ignore it. He made no attempt to start a conversation as they passed between the members of the household and the other guests, who had moved aside to make a passage for the family to leave the chapel. Outside, he walked beside her across the yard and into the house, but still, to her irritation, he said nothing. She resolved to punish him, but that meant that she would have to speak first.

"I'm going to my quarters now, Sir John, so we must part. It seems you have nought to say to me, in spite of seeking my company."

"Ah, my lady, I'm unable to speak. My heart is so full of love for you that it's blocking my throat and preventing words from escaping."

She giggled, and pleasure brightened her eyes. Impulsively, her shoulders hunched and she looked straight at him. "Sir John, I've never heard such fine words from you before. Are you turning into a poet?"

"Not I! And yet I swear I could wield words as skilfully as a sword, if I willed. Or if a beautiful lady so desired."

Patrina's body almost shimmered in her delight at having drawn such emotions from John. "I hope you find such a beautiful lady," she whispered archly.

"I trow I have found her. I think perhaps it's a vision I'm walking beside. Can she be real?" He sighed so loudly that she glanced at him, although she never suspected that it was deliberate. "But I fear she may love another, and so I will have to ride away with a broken heart."

"Oh, Sir John, don't say that. Please don't. I would that you stayed." She was truly sorry to feel that she would be responsible for such sadness, because she believed his words implicitly. Her eyes were modestly downcast, damp with a touch of tears, and so she did not see the satisfied smile on his face as he spoke again.

"Very well, my lady. I'll stay, and I pray I may sit near you at dinner."

Before she could answer, her aunt, who had been walking a step in front of them, turned and told Patrina that she desired her help in her room. She motioned to her and told her to come immediately, so Patrina threw John a helpless smile and fell into step beside her aunt. She was not too unhappy at the intervention, because she thought that it might be good to keep John dangling a little. He had shown that he still loved her, and she was satisfied with that.

When Patrina was awoken by her maid on St. Stephen's Day, it was to be told that there had been snow in the night. It was not a great deal, being little more than an inch in depth, but it covered everything closely and hid the grime and squalor of the everyday with a pure brightness. After breakfast Patrina went to her room and put on warm outdoor clothing, ready to join the hunt which had been arranged for that morning.

At the stables the men had prepared horses for the party and they were soon all mounted and trotting out into the country. When they came into woodland, the party began to split, as paths were found through the trees. Patrina soon found herself riding with John. Excited but wary, her spirits rose. It came into her head to chaff him, for they had found no prey yet. She knew that it would make him angry, but she wanted the danger of teasing him. She could hear the dogs some distance away, and guessed from the tone of their baying that they had started up a stag. It pleased her that John was torn between being with them and being with her, and she gripped her reins more tightly.

Through the grey-black trees, she saw her father. He too had become separated from the main party and was now spurring his horse to rejoin the hounds. Taking pity on John, Patrina drew his attention and was about to suggest that they follow her father, when she saw her father's head strike a branch. Stunned, he tumbled off his horse. She screamed her alarm, but John was already on his way, weaving through the trees. Quick as he was, however, a wild boar was quicker. Disturbed by all the activity in the wood, it came charging down a narrow path, directly towards the earl. Without faltering, the boar continued. The disoriented earl had rolled over onto his hands and knees. He lifted his head, but had no time to do anything else as the boar caught him side-on. One tusk ripped through his overtunic and into his shoulder. The second went into his side. Patrina, forcing her way quickly through the wood, saw her father roll over. At the sight, a hot breath caught in her throat, as she thought that he was about to be killed. The boar pulled its shoulders back and prepared to gouge again. As it did, John's horse clattered up to it. John leaped off with a shout, and, distracted, the boar turned its head, peering with its narrow eyes. It was too late. John grabbed a tusk with his left hand. Jerking the head upwards with as much strength as he could muster, he thrust the knife in his right hand into the boar's neck. Seemingly in one movement, he twisted the knife and slashed. As hot blood spurted out over the earl, John began to pull the still-struggling animal backwards. He hacked again with his knife. The boar rolled over onto its back, and although John was hit by one of the trotters, he drove the knife into the boar's chest.

Patrina had dismounted by now. Fearfully skirting the struggle between the man and the weakening beast, she hurried to her father. He had managed to sit up, but Patrina was almost overcome at the sight of all the blood that covered him. She did not know that much of it was from the boar and, weeping profusely in her anguish, she pulled off her mantle, thinking that she must try to staunch the blood. Suddenly John was kneeling beside her and she realised that the noise of the fight with the boar had ended. Even the horses were quiet, although still skittish.

John raised his head and gave a shout for assistance, and then another. The earl's groom soon appeared, quickly followed by other people. Patrina was relieved to let John take charge. She allowed herself to be escorted gently away from her father by one of the other ladies, and she watched as John examined her father's wounds. The old man was conscious and somewhat grumbly at the interruption to his hunting.

"Can't you get me up onto my horse again, Sir John? Have they got that stag yet? I'm missing the kill."

"Gently, my lord. I fear me you're sorely wounded. We must get you home."

"'Sblood! I've had worse. I can't let it spoil my day."

In a way, Patrina was glad to hear him complain, because she hoped it meant that he was not too seriously hurt. However, she could see that his normally florid face had turned a pasty white, so she knelt by him and wiped his brow with her kerchief. Worry pulled at her forehead as she also said that he must go home. She turned her head to where John was organising the construction of a makeshift stretcher with a cloak and two poles. "Hurry, Sir John. I beg of you to hurry," she cried.

Despite his continuing grumbles, the earl was lifted onto the stretcher and carried back to the road. The man whom John had sent for a horse and cart was already waiting, and Patrina rode back with her father, cradling his head in her lap.

Back at the house, his wounds were soon dressed and, propped up in bed, he called for John to come and see him.

John brought the head of the boar to show him, marching proudly through the doorway. "Here you are, my lord! What think you of him now?"

The earl chortled at the fate which had befallen his attacker. "He's not so fierce now, I ween."

"No, my lord. And so perish all your enemies."

Patrina, sitting demurely by the bed, looked wonderingly at the splashes of blood which could still be seen on John's tunic, even though he had taken off his outer clothes and washed his hands. In her mind's eye she could still see how he had grabbed the boar and killed it. That was real bravery, not an arranged fight with another knight. How romantic! But what a pity, she thought, that it had been her father whom John had rescued and not she. Though she would not like to have been hurt – just to have been in danger. That would have been exciting.

She listened to her father praising John's bravery and skill, and she also praised him. Relief at her father's rescue seemed to colour everything around her. John agreed with their praises and willingly described what had happened, as if the other two had not been there. Patrina helped him with the description, and joined in the laughter as all three relaxed in the safety of the afternoon.

Then her father turned towards her. "Sir John is the man for you to marry, my dear. He's the son for me. He'd be a fine husband, would he not?"

"He is a fine man, Father. I say also that he would be a fine husband for a fortunate lady."

"I grant he would, my dear. He's the knight you should wed. Sending knights off to gather flowers is only romantic nonsense."

"But, Father, I promised Sir Carlyon that I would make no decision until he returned."

"The decision is mine, not yours. How long can we wait? What say you, Sir John?"

"I say that Sir Carlyon is a fine and brave knight, my lord. He's undertaken a dangerous journey to go and gather a few flowers, I ween, but how long will it take?" John shrugged. "It may be many months before he returns. Mayhap he never will return. Will my lady grow old and grey while waiting for him?"

The earl laughed, as if that idea were fanciful. Patrina lowered her eyes and looked thoughtfully at the floor. She was suddenly nervous at the turn which events had taken. Her feelings for Carlyon unexpectedly made her heart bump. He was kind and gentle and he treated her like a lady on a pedestal. Surely Sir John was not the better man? What was she to do?

Her father seemed to guess that she needed a prod. "We can't wait and wait," he said gruffly. "I'll send to my lord Cerre-nore and discuss it with him. If he is agreeable to his son's betrothal, we'll make the arrangements."

# 11

Meanwhile, Carlyon had decided to make changes to his own arrangements. After his decision to turn eastwards, he, James and Mary had travelled on in good spirits along a road that was reasonably open, albeit miry and uneven. This took them to a small town called Stockport, where they spent a night. In the morning, while he dressed, Carlyon considered which direction to take. It would be easy, from where they were, to go round the north of the forest in which Thomas lived. That route would also take them close to where Mary's brother lived. That would discharge Carlyon's obligation to Mary and let him continue with what he had been called to do. The task was his duty and must be completed.

He looked over at his window, where the servant had opened the shutter when he'd brought in the jug of hot water. The grey light of the early morning struggled in weakly. It made the room seem cold, and Carlyon began to think about the witch. He wondered where she was. Perhaps she was no longer pursuing them? Was the sword *so* important to her? He chewed his lip. He could not take the chance. Standing there, he shivered, even though he was now fully dressed. He well remembered the effect she had had on him at the tavern in Aylesbury. There had been evil in her very presence. He had felt it then. He could feel it now. Perhaps she was not so far away? She could come upon them at any time.

When he saw the other two at breakfast, he explained his concerns to them and put forward a proposal. "I intend to take a wide circle to get to the Wirral. If we go north-eastwards and then come round again, we can approach from the north. That'll be safer, because the witch won't be expecting that."

James nodded, seeming perfectly agreeable.

Carlyon looked at Mary, who had put her thumb tip between her teeth, as if to help her to think. Before she could say anything, he said, "You'll be safe in Stockport, Mary, until you can find a carrier travelling towards your brother's house. Then you'll be able to get home."

She seemed disappointed at his words. "I doubt there'll be many people travelling in midwinter," she said. "I don't know what I'll do while I'm waiting."

"I can give you some money for lodging. I'm only thinking that your family will be worried about you." He paused and looked at her. He could see the worry in her eyes, and abruptly he made a decision. "No. Perhaps it would not be good for a young maid to be alone. You can travel with us, if you would prefer to do that. 'Twill only be a few extra days, I ween."

"Please, sir, I'd feel safer under your protection. I'll travel with you awhile yet, and perhaps I may be of help to you."

Carlyon smiled at her. He was unexpectedly pleased at her decision, and he sent James out to acquire a saddle for the packhorse. However, when they came to repack their things, they found it impossible to distribute everything evenly. In the end, Carlyon said that they would carry on as they had, with Mary travelling on Champion behind him. He was not too unhappy with that, and he told himself that any pleasurable thoughts he had about Mary were totally harmless. She was a pleasant woman who had shown herself to be kind and capable. It crossed his mind that perhaps he would ask her if she wanted to go south with him, after he had found the flowers of the swan. She could enter his service after he was married to Patrina and had his own household.

When they left Stockport, Carlyon led them to the east, although under the grey snow-laden clouds he mistakenly thought that he was going more northwards than eastwards. The terrain became rougher as they rode into the High Peak, and they were lucky to find shelter for the night. On awaking the next morning, they found that it was snowing and travel was impossible. Carlyon, irritated at his wrong decision, spent the day in a bad mood. He only recovered some good spirits late in the afternoon, when Mary prepared him a hot drink infused with herbs and spices. She also tried to console him.

"I'm sure we'll be able to travel tomorrow. The snow's already falling not so heavily."

"I don't know. There are so many delays. I only pray the snow is holding up the witch also."

That proved to be scant comfort when the snow blew itself out only late in the afternoon of the following day. It was too late to set off, but Carlyon and James went out to survey things. Carlyon was pleased to find that the snow was in fact not too deep, apart from in places where the wind had blown it into drifts. Mostly it was little more than shin-deep; less than a large hand's span. The main problem was that all the tracks and landmarks were covered. As Carlyon looked round at the stark beauty that draped the hills about him, he realised that their journey could be slow and uncertain.

"How will we find our way, sire?" asked James, screwing up his face in thought as he also looked around.

"I don't know. We must trust in God and our good fortune."

"Will we be able to find our way back to Stockport? We can find a road from there, I trow."

"Yes, but I wish not to go back to where we've been. I think we might try to go off that way." Carlyon pointed optimistically in what he thought was a north-westerly direction.

James looked at the snow-locked landscape, but made no comment.

Carlyon looked back at the holes their steps had made in the snow, and wondered how the horses would cope. Then he looked up at the sky and tried to guess whether any more snow was likely. "There seems to be an unlucky fate placing handicaps in my way," he muttered, more to himself than to James. "There's been delay after delay and now we've got this snow."

"It's not *all* been unlucky. We've rescued Mary."

"Of course. That's the one good thing, although I would rather Thomas had not taken her and we had not had to spend the time." Carlyon paused, caught by James's concerned look. "Mistake me not. I'm glad we've rescued her and I wouldn't have left her there. It's just that – oh, I don't know!" His teeth were clamped together in irritation and he looked round as if he wanted to throw something, but any stick or stone was covered by snow. "What am I doing wrong?" he asked, seemingly of the surrounding hills. "Why is it so difficult? Is it because I forgot to scatter the corn for the swans? How am I going to do that now?"

"Perhaps it's the corn that's bringing you bad luck and you should get rid of it?"

"Think you so? Yes, mayhap. But no. It was blessed by a holy man. Surely it can't be cursed. I'll keep it yet." Then, bethinking himself that speaking his pessimistic thoughts aloud was not good for James, who would be expecting leadership, Carlyon quickly said, "Ho, James, we can't do anything more out here. We'll go back and prepare for departure. We must leave on the morrow."

The following daybreak, Carlyon felt that there had been a slight rise in temperature during the night. As they prepared to leave, he noticed some drips of water falling from the eaves of the stable roof. He hoped that that was a good sign, and he got into his saddle with a lighter heart than when he had awoken. Once Mary was behind him, they set off, guided for most of the morning by a local shepherd. When they stopped for dinner, the shepherd left them, saying that he had to go back to see to his flock, which was scattered over the hills. Before he went, he pointed out their way, and it was with some reluctance that Carlyon watched him start on his trudge back.

They had not travelled far that morning. Nor did they travel great distances over the succeeding days. The soft snow slowed their progress considerably, and in places where it was thawing there were treacherous pools and slippery sludge that had to be traversed with care. Often they had to dismount and lead the horses.

One evening, when they had managed to find accommodation in a Cistercian monastery, Carlyon sat in his small room and considered what to do next. His plan had been to go a fair way north along the Pennines and then strike west, before turning south to reach the Wirral across the River Mersey.

It was a large circle, but he had calculated that it would not take long if they were able to make good speed. However, the skies had been consistently overcast. They had had barely six hours of good daylight for travelling each day. As a result, they were not so far along as he had expected and hoped. Precious time was being wasted. He resolved that he must make the best of it and turn towards the west when they set off on the morrow. While he was thinking over that decision, he suddenly thought to hear a voice in his ear. His shield was speaking. Carlyon gave a start. It had been so long since that had happened that he had almost convinced himself that it had been a dream. Now, in the gloomy light of his rush, he looked at the shield.

"Time is passing," it told him. "The witch has discovered that she has been tricked. She is on her way after you."

"That's not good. We can't seem to go any faster."

"The witch is not far behind you. You must make all haste on the morrow. Continue in the same direction. It will be difficult for the witch in these hills."

Then the sonorous voice drifted away like smoke from the rushlight and the shield was as immobile as ever. Despondency was a cold cloak on Carlyon's back as he sat there and contemplated what he had just heard. It seemed pointless to continue. However, sleeping on it loosened the cloak slightly and he determined to follow the shield's advice.

When he met up with the other two over breakfast, he was in a positive mood. "We're being pursued by the witch. My plan failed. I'm going to press on, but she could catch up at any time. She's not interested in either of you. If I go on alone, I'll be able to travel faster and so I may escape her. The two of you can cut off safely and, James, you will be able to guide Mary to her brother's house."

"I don't want to leave you alone, sire," said James. "If the witch catches up with you, it'll be better if there are two of us."

Mary had been listening quietly to Carlyon's proposal, the tip of her thumb placed thoughtfully between her teeth. Now she turned away and went to the bag which held her things. He thought that she had accepted his plan and was already preparing to leave. Disappointment rose in his throat and he had to swallow. He had made a serious proposal, but he would have preferred not to have had to make it. It had been a pleasure to have Mary sitting behind him and holding him close for warmth. He pulled nonchalance into his features and prepared to tell James that his decision was final. But before he could speak, Mary turned back to them, holding a small casket.

"I agree with James," she said. "This witch won't be defeated by just one person alone." She opened the casket and took out a small leather pouch. "I've taken this from Thomas. It contains a special sand. If we sprinkle it on the ground behind us, it'll help us, I'm sure."

Carlyon was about to argue, but there was something in the steely determination of Mary's voice and the way that she stood which made him hesitate. On an impulse, he decided to trust her. "Very well – we stay together. Come, then, we'll be away."

They travelled on, making good time for once, as the track seemed easier. This both pleased and worried Carlyon, because he thought that if they were doing well, then the witch too would move with the same ease. Nevertheless, they pressed on and eventually came to a narrow pass which led them over a moor.

At this point, he felt Mary move away from him as she looked back. "I think this will be a good place to scatter the sand," she said.

Carlyon looked at her and saw reassurance in her beautiful blue eyes. He would do it. He let James and the packhorse pass. Then he opened the pouch. Slowly, he let the sand fall out, scattering it as widely as he could. He spurred Champion on, and when he looked back after a minute or so, he saw that behind them the snow was growing thicker and deeper. Soon there was a large drift which completely blocked the way. Feeling slightly relieved, he carried on, and still their way seemed easier.

After two more days he judged it safe enough to turn westwards and take a track which led them out of the hills. He was not sure where he was, but after another day's travel they awoke to skies that were no longer cloudy. The sunlight was strong, but gave little warmth. Even so, it enlightened their spirits, and when Carlyon saw higher ground crowding the western horizon before them, he felt that it was time to turn southwards. They continued through the fells, Carlyon keeping a watchful eye on the sky. He was thankful that there was no sign of more snow for them. The clear skies were keeping the already fallen snow crisp and hard, and although it was at times slippery, the horses moved with reasonable ease. Carlyon began to look forward to getting out of the wilderness through which they were travelling and onto a proper highway. He had a feeling that his journey's end was in sight.

Late one afternoon they were preparing for that night's rest in a shepherd's shelter which they had come across. James was out gathering more wood for the fire. Mary was just outside, skinning and preparing two hares which Carlyon had bought from a trapper whom they had met on the moor. Carlyon was sitting on the floor by the fire and idly keeping an eye on a pot of water which Mary had put on to boil, when he was interrupted by the softly insistent voice of the shield, which spoke as if directly into his ear.

"Time is passing. You need not have gone so far north into Westmorland. You will have to make haste now. The witch is still behind you and she is catching up."

"I thought we'd stopped her."

"The sand Mary gave you performed its task well. It delayed the witch. She had to use her hot breath to melt her way through the snow, and that has weakened her. But she is through the snow now and she is hastening after you again. She is less than a day behind."

"Uh-oh!" The sound which came out of Carlyon's mouth was part sigh and part groan. "We must indeed make haste. But our horses need to rest tonight. We too must conserve our strength. I know we'll have need of it."

It was not until they were sitting to eat the stew which Mary had made that Carlyon told them about the witch's passage through the snow. James seemed surprised, but it was not clear to Carlyon whether it was surprise that the witch had got through the snow or that Carlyon should know about it.

"I can sense the witch's malevolence," Carlyon told them. "So we must lose no time in leaving on the morrow."

James had picked up a piece of meat, which he was holding by the bone, ready to gnaw, but he continued to hold it in his hand while listening to Carlyon. He looked unhappily across at him and said, "We've been travelling too slowly. We should have parted when you suggested."

"That can't be helped. We've got where we are and we're still safe. We'll be off this moor after tomorrow, I'm sure of it. We're not far from Blackburn now, and there'll be a firm road after that."

Mary had remained silent during this exchange. Carlyon looked at her with his head slightly to one side, wondering what she was thinking. She smiled at him, and despite himself, he seemed to feel a bright light burst up inside him. Without thought, she had become part of his life and he was beginning to treat her little differently from how he treated James. She bowed her head modestly under his gaze, as if she understood his feelings, and then quietly, almost hesitantly, she spoke.

"I'm truly grateful for your protection, sir. I too can sense this witch's malevolence, but I'm sure we can defeat her. I have something in my casket which I think will be able to help us. I'll get it out on the morrow."

Carlyon's heart lifted at her words, thinking that more deep snow behind them might buy them enough time to reach the Wirral. He wanted to reach over and take her hand in gratitude. Had she not been merely a thatcher's daughter, he would have done so. He thanked her in words, and she went back to her food with barely a sigh.

The next morning they were awake just before dawn. As Carlyon looked eastwards after having stepped outside, he could see streaks of cloud along the hills being backlit by the sun, which was about to haul itself up into the sky. He wondered where the witch was and whether she had been travelling through the night. Perhaps they should not have waited until sunrise. His musings were interrupted by Mary's emergence from the shelter. Realising without words that she wanted to be private, he snapped into movement and went back into the shelter. Inside, he looked over at the bags and remembered that she had said that she had something in her casket to delay the witch. He told himself that it was fortunate that she had kept back some of the magic sand. If the snow delayed the witch for as long as before, that should give them enough time.

When the horses were saddled and loaded, Carlyon prepared to mount Champion, but Mary asked him to wait. She had been for a walk a few yards away while he and James had been getting the horses ready, and he looked at her in surprise. He'd assumed that she had been engaged in some private woman's toilet, and he had respected her modesty. Now he could not think why she was delaying them when speed was important, but he put his foot back on the ground. He was sure that she would have a good reason.

"We need to use this before we leave."

As she spoke, she pulled a small wooden stick out of her cloak. It was little more than a span in length, and no thicker than a maiden's finger. She offered it to him and he took it, turning it in his fingers curiously, so that he could look all over it. There seemed to be nothing special about it. Would this be better than the sand?

"I took it from Thomas," she said. "You must poke it in the ground and it'll help us. I've found a suitable place over there. I'll show you."

Carlyon followed where she led, but when she stopped and he looked around, he could see nothing out of the ordinary. They were out of the lee of the slope where their night's shelter had been, and the snow-covered moor stretched openly before them. There was little to be seen in the growing dawn light, except for scattered mounds where the snow sheeted leafless bushes. Momentarily, he was assailed by doubt. Surely this would not be a good place to bring snow? It was too open. He watched as Mary used her hands to clear the snow from a small patch at their feet. The snow there was only a shallow sprinkling, and a circle of dark earth was quickly visible.

"Poke the stick into that," she told him.

"I'll try," he said, ignoring the note of command in her voice, thinking more that the ground might be frostbound and too hard to penetrate with such a flimsy stick. He crouched and, looking for a spot that might be easiest, pushed one end of the stick into the soil. To his surprise, it went in straight away; almost as if something were pulling it out of his hand. It went about halfway down its length and then stopped. He pushed a little more, but it would not move. He stood up and looked at Mary. "Is that it?" he asked.

"Yes. Come, sir, let's move away."

They backed off, but nothing happened. Then, as they moved even farther, the stick began to grow. It sprouted twigs, then branches. Quickly the bush spread upwards and sideways. Before long, it was an impenetrable thicket of wood and thorns that stretched in a line over the moor, seemingly for miles to either side of them. Carlyon watched, unable to move. He thought at first that it would go up to reach the sky, but he judged it to be only the height of two men on horseback when it stopped growing. He looked along the hedge in both directions. It was impossible to see through it, and he stepped forward, intending to go for a closer look, but he felt Mary tug at his sleeve.

"We must leave now, sir. Time is passing."

Her words held him more firmly than her hand on his sleeve, and he nodded. Without a word he led the way back to the horses, unheeding that, until then, it had been Mary who had been leading him.

Two days later, they were crossing the stark, treeless waste of the Belmont moors. Carlyon's optimism had been misplaced. There had been more snow, and accordingly their pace had slowed. They halted for dinner at an inn, and Carlyon spoke to the landlord about their chances of making it to Bolton le Moors before nightfall. The landlord was doubtful, even though the snow clouds had blown away. Carlyon pursed his lips, unsure whether the man was looking for extra business if he and his party stayed the night. He went outside and looked up at the sky. It told him nothing. He went to the stable and looked at the horses. They were having a feed of corn, and to Carlyon's eye they looked fresh enough to carry on through the afternoon. If there was no more snow to come, then he was certain that they could be off the moors in less than two hours. He patted Champion's neck and told him to eat up, because they would soon be on their way. As he let his arm fall, he glanced at his shield, fastened to his saddle, and saw that the boss had turned into a face.

The voice came almost immediately. "Time is passing. The witch is furious. The hedge proved impassable. She tried to get through it. She tried to climb over it. She tried to cut it down. But nothing worked for her. So she has had to travel round it. This has taken her time and weakened her yet more, but the hedge was not endless and at last she is back on your trail."

"Then we must leave straight away and make all haste possible."

"That is so. But leave the highway."

The voice disappeared into the shadows and Champion stamped his feet restlessly, making his harness rattle. The shield was featureless again. Carlyon glanced up over his saddle to meet the eyes of the stable boy, whom he had paid to watch over their belongings. The boy was sitting in some straw for warmth at the side of the stable, and had been watching him. Carlyon patted Champion's neck and muttered some endearment to him, intending to give the boy the impression that he had just been talking to his horse. Smiling a little wryly, he went back into the inn and told the other two that the witch was close behind them again.

"We'll leave now and go across the moor before it gets dark." He scratched at his furrowed brow with one of his hands and said, as if thinking aloud, "I don't know what we can do to stop this witch. She just keeps coming and coming."

James looked at Mary and asked, "Do you have anything which will help us again? I pray you, Mary, that you'll have something. You're our only hope."

Carlyon jerked sharply out of his despondent introspection and also looked at Mary, jealous that James had asked for her help when he himself had not thought to do so. Now, as she looked back at him, his trusting hope seemed to illuminate her face with a gentle light. And yet, despite all that they had been through, he was still unaware of the love that she had for him, and of the powers it was giving her. For a second or two she looked at him, and then she switched her gaze to James, seemingly disappointed that Carlyon had not sought her aid. It appeared to Carlyon that her face darkened, as if turning her head had moved it into shadow. Momentarily he wished that she were not so far beneath him in rank, but the wish was so fleeting that it was barely formed in his mind. He leaned forward slightly, so as not to miss any of the words which Mary's quiet voice was now speaking.

"I have something in my casket. Because this woman is a witch, she will be afraid of fire. I have a flint that will make a fire to keep her away. You will have to stay behind to strike it."

Carlyon now realised why she had been speaking to James rather than to him. However, he was not happy about leaving such a task to James, who was his squire and so was his responsibility to protect. It would be a dangerous matter for a callow youth. "Is that so?" he asked, placing authority carefully into his voice. "We've come thus far together. Can we not strike this flint of yours as we travel, and so keep the witch at bay? James is my squire and I must answer to his father for his well-being. I like not that I should leave him behind. There may be other services he can render me."

"This service will be a great one, sir. And a necessary one. The witch must be kept in one place by fire, to give you time to get away. It has to be constant, so that it takes away her powers. I'll know where to do it. Have no fear: James will be perfectly safe if he follows my instructions."

Carlyon's back stiffened at the implication of command in her words, but immediately he realised that he had nothing else to suggest. Resuming his authority, he called to the landlord for the reckoning and told James to go and prepare the horses.

Outside the village, Carlyon led them off the highway and across the moor to a hill which he could see a few miles in the distance. To his surprise they made good time, and he was just beginning to wonder where Mary would choose to hold the witch when he felt her press his arm.

"I think we should stop here," she said. "There's a small space under that rock where James can shelter."

Carlyon looked where she was pointing. He too saw what she had spotted: the black shape of what was almost a cave. Mary slipped down from behind him, and he also dismounted. They went to look, followed by James. The space was dry and easily large enough for James to wait there without too much discomfort.

Carlyon turned to look at him. "I'd fain stay myself, rather than you, if only it were possible. But by Our Lord's grace, you'll be safe."

"I'll do my best, sire. There's no other help for it."

Carlyon looked at him fondly, but before he could say anything more, Mary returned from the horses with her little casket. She took out a flint and stone and showed James how to strike it.

"Strike it when the witch draws close enough for you to see her eyes. Strike again each time the fire begins to die down. Gradually the witch will grow weaker. You'll know to stop and leave this place to come after us when the witch is no longer moving. God keep you safe, and we'll see you again."

# 12

James stood and watched his master ride away with Mary holding on behind him. With his fists clenched, he tried to fight back the superstitious sense of loneliness which engulfed him. He had not wanted to stay behind. Fear of the witch and nervousness at being alone on the moor had made his heart race and his limbs seem to tremble, but Mary had smiled at him so sweetly that his veins seemed to fill with a roaring courage. She was three or so years older than he was, and although he was of a higher rank, her calm competence made him look on her as second only to Carlyon; almost as if she and Carlyon were master and mistress. But now Mary was gone, and James would have to face whatever danger was approaching with no help, except for his faith in her words.

He looked around, but there was no sign of life. His horse was hobbled out of sight and he too would have to hide himself. He exhaled in acceptance and went into his shelter. Sitting on his saddle with his cloak wrapped round him, he saw that Mary had chosen well. He was completely sheltered, but he had a good view of the way along which the witch would come. He pulled his hood tightly round his face, so that only a few strands of hair peeped out, and settled down to wait.

The time passed slowly. James seemed to be in a wilderness. The shadowed hollows of the rocky moorland were filled with silence. No travellers came by. No shepherd or drover could be seen. There were no animals, except for the birds that occasionally flew by, and once he saw a fox sauntering across the snow. From time to time he stretched out his legs or stood up to look around. At the beginning of his vigil he had been constantly alert; constantly scanning the moor between him and the horizon, where the distant Pennines fluted the sky's lower edges. As veiled evening began to stroll solitary down those eastern hills, James's attention began to falter.

Then he saw movement. The sun was behind cloud, low to the south-west, and the eastern side of the moor was becoming dark. James's heart pounded and a hot spear of anxiety poked his throat. He had been worrying about spending the night in this lonely place. Now he was more worried about what the witch might do and whether he would be able to cope. He strained his eyes to make out the movement. It may not have been the witch...but he knew that it was. Gradually he saw a shape form, and as it grew nearer, it became human. Nearer still and he was able to make out that it was a woman, wrapped in a hooded black cloak that covered all of her body and left only her face exposed. Without realising it, James was barely breathing, held fascinated while the witch came closer. Her horse seemed to be flitting over the snow, leaving no track that he could see; almost as if its hooves were not touching the ground. James wondered at first whether she were flying. Then suddenly he was jerked into awareness, as if the flint in his hand had become hot. He looked down at it, and got ready with the stone in his other hand. When he looked up again, he was horrified to find the witch almost upon him. He could see her eyes piercing into his head.

Frantically, he struck the flint. He had no idea what would happen. For a moment he doubted that a mere spark could have any effect on the witch's progress. But he had faith in Mary, and so he struck. A flame spurted out to hit the snow in front of the witch. Safe in his shelter, James watched. Her horse reared, throwing off the witch. As it skittered away across the moor, the flame spread, encircling the witch almost instantaneously. Although several yards away, James could feel the heat and see the snow beginning to melt and boil where the fire touched it. He wondered if the witch would be consumed, but disappointment gripped him as he saw through the flames that her powers were able to protect her from that fate. But that was all that they could do. James watched as she jumped about in the small circle, seemingly trying to overcome the flames. Nothing worked. She was able neither to put out the fire, nor to get through it. Then, as darkness fell, the flames began to die down. James carefully struck the flint on its stone, and to his relief the fire was renewed with its former intensity.

At last the witch called to him. "Young boy, let me out of here! Come now, let me out!"

"No. You have to stay there until the time has passed."

"I don't mean you any harm. Let me out."

"You mean to harm my master, I'm sure of it."

"No, I won't harm him. I only want my property back and then I'll leave you alone. Let me out, I'm like to burn here. Don't let me perish."

"Stop jumping about and you'll be safe. I'll let you out when the time comes."

James struck the flint again and the witch screamed as the flames reared up fiercely anew. When she spoke again, her cajoling tone had been replaced with an anger that seemed to leap through the fire to try to reach James.

"You'll pay for this, you stubborn boy. If you don't let me out, it'll be the worse for you!"

This time James did not answer. The witch threatened and pleaded by turns for a little while more, but James remained silent. In the end the witch also fell silent, although by the light of the flames he could see her darting about in her circular prison until gradually she grew weaker. As time passed, his confidence in the flint's magical powers grew. He was sure that he would be able to hold her.

When Carlyon and Mary had left James, they'd carried on across the moor. Towards the evening they had reached a road and, travelling along it, come upon an abandoned cottage in an overgrown copse. Most of the roof was missing, but the walls were sound and Mary suggested that they rest there for the night. Carlyon disagreed, wanting to carry on in order to put more distance between them and the witch.

"It'll be safe to stay here, so long as James keeps the witch surrounded by fire," Mary told him. "So long as he keeps striking the flint, the witch will grow weaker, and by morning she'll be unable to follow us."

Carlyon looked at her thoughtfully, but he had no reason to doubt her. He wanted to trust her. Nodding his head, he looked round to survey the cottage. "It's as good a place as any," he said. "I wonder why it's empty."

"The people will have died of sickness, I'll warrant. But it was many years ago."

"Died? There may be spirits about here, then."

"There'll be nought to wish us harm. We can sleep here."

He let her slip to the ground, and then he dismounted himself. Taking the horses to the side of the cottage, he prepared them for the night. He was just about to pick up the pouches to take them into the cottage when he had a sudden thought. Perhaps he should hide the sword? He stood a few seconds more in thought. Why had that idea come into his head? Was there danger nearby? Looking round in the twilight, he saw nothing. Yes, he thought to himself. It may be good to hide the sword. He glanced upwards and saw that he could push the sword's scabbard into the thatch under the eaves. Once it was there, it was completely unnoticeable, the roof being in such a straggly state of disrepair that it was difficult to see where Carlyon had disturbed it.

He carried their bags into the cottage and went out again to help Mary, who was gathering some firewood. While he got a fire going, she cleared out a space near one of the walls under the least dilapidated part of the roof. By the time darkness had fallen, they had a warm, cheerful light to keep them company. Carlyon sat on his saddle by the fire and looked up at the night sky. Then he looked over at Mary, who was sitting cross-legged on the floor by him. She smiled at him.

"We could have carried on," he said. "This road would surely have led us to an inn."

"I think not. I know this area and we would have had to travel into the night before finding lodgings. We'll be comfortable enough here and we can leave at dawn tomorrow. My mother lives no more than two days' journey from here. It'll be good to rest there."

"I don't know if I'll have the time. If the witch recovers her strength…"

"That may happen, but my mother will be a match for her. My mother has many powerful forces for good. You'll see. She'll be able to protect us." Mary paused and looked down at the floor between them, then spoke, as if nonchalantly. "My mother will be able to advise you on your search for the flowers of the swan. If you still want to continue."

"Of course! I've come this far and I'll go on. I must find the flowers and take them back to my lady. I made her a vow and I'll keep it. My lady will be waiting for me and expecting me to return with the flowers. I won't disappoint her."

He looked at Mary and smiled at her fondly and almost regretfully. It was strange that he should be speaking so familiarly to a peasant, and yet fate had drawn them together. They had each rendered the other great service and he would be sorry if she was unable to become a servant in his household. He had been impressed by her simple beauty and her quiet, competent ways, and he could not prevent himself from comparing them to Patrina's made-up beauty and romantic dreams. He almost regretted that the differences in their stations in life made him unable to give his hand to Mary and take hers. However, even if they had been equal, he had declared his love to Patrina. He would keep his word and stay faithful to her. It was his duty to do that. As these fleeting thoughts passed through his mind, he failed to notice the wistfulness in the look Mary was giving him, before she turned her head to gaze into the fire. She knew that she had to be patient, and as he looked at her slightly bowed head, he sensed how her presence was filling the cottage's single room with calm and contentment. After a while Mary moved to put some more wood on the fire, and Carlyon was stirred into thinking of a meal.

"We must eat now. We have bread and meat."

"No, sir. I think it will be best not to eat tonight. We must fast until morning. Then we'll be strong in spirit for what may happen in the night and what still lies ahead of us."

"We'll be strong enough. A light supper will be good."

"It will be harm. We must leave aside such bodily desires this night and strengthen our minds for a battle yet to come."

He looked at her, not totally convinced. He could not think what else more arduous could lie before them, if the witch was held at bay. Mary was watching him with a hand to her mouth and the knuckle of her forefinger between her lips. She seemed to be waiting anxiously for what he would do. For a few seconds he sat with his lips pressed together in thought. There was something about his companion that was making him pause. Truly, he had never before met such a peasant. Her self-possession was weaving silken bonds round his limbs. He wondered suddenly whether the differences between lords and peasants were more contrived than natural. Almost before he knew what he was doing, he nodded. He would accept her advice, and although he said nothing, he saw her body relax as she guessed what he had decided. She reached out to pull one of the pouches nearer, so that she could use it as a pillow, and wrapped her cloak closely about her.

"I'll sleep now," she said. "If you also sleep, you'll not feel your hunger. The morrow will be here before we know it."

In truth, he was not feeling very hungry. They had eaten well at midday and so he was prepared to settle down for the night.

But he was not yet sleepy. He reached over and idly moved some of the sticks which were jutting out from the fire. Sparks flew up and part of the fire collapsed with a short crash, drawing Mary's attention, but Carlyon sat back and everything settled down again. He wrapped his cloak round him and stayed as he was: sitting on his saddle and looking into the fire.

His thoughts moved to where James too would be sitting on his saddle, all alone. Perhaps he was too young to have been given such an important task. Carlyon's brow furrowed as fingers of anxiety pulled at it. But there was no one else, unless Mary had stayed. For a few seconds he toyed with that notion, thinking that she might have been more able to control the witch. But she had not wanted to stay behind, even though it had been she who had provided the flint. It had almost been as if she had been leading and making the decisions for the three of them. He looked down at her, already asleep, lying wrapped in her cloak with only her head showing. Her long light brown hair looked black in the uncertain light from the fire. He wondered what it would be like were it fastened up as a married woman's and covered with a silken veil. And if she were dressed all in richly dyed silk and damask, would she be in her appearance no different from a lady? But she would not be a lady. Not as Patrina was. She could not read or write. She could not... Here he paused, as he wondered what else Mary could not do that Lady Patrina could. Could she weave and sew? Could she sit at table and eat fine food with delicate refinement? Could she play backgammon? Well, no doubt she could learn such accomplishments. They were acquired, not inbred. But would that make a peasant into a lady? Why should it not? he asked himself.

He moved his head from side to side, as a vision of Patrina strode into his mind and pushed Mary aside. He wondered what

Patrina was doing at that moment. Still in the hall, watching an after-supper entertainment? In her chamber with her maid, being prepared for bed? Or perhaps already in bed? He looked up at the sky through the damaged roof and sent his fond dreams to her, hoping that she would be thinking of him as he was thinking of her. He wished he was back at her father's house; able to sleep in a proper bed. Instead he was in an abandoned labourer's cottage on the edge of a Lancashire moor, spending the night alone with a peasant woman who had in such a short time almost become a part of his life. He looked around the gloomy place in which he was to sleep, and then down at Mary. He would never have thought such a thing possible.

Determination suddenly gripped his shoulders, pulling his spine straight. Time was passing and it was surely growing shorter. He must lose no more of it. This would be his final delay. At dawn tomorrow he would head straight for the Wirral and find the flowers of the swan. Then he could return in triumph to Lady Patrina and claim her hand in marriage, before Sir John could do so. Fired by those thoughts, he nodded his satisfaction. Bodily sensations returned. He could feel the cold on his back. Stiffness in his legs made him stretch them out. He realised also that he was hungry, as if all his thinking and dreaming had taken up energy. The thought of the meat in his pouch brought saliva into his mouth. It would be good to keep up his strength with a little food. However, he remembered what Mary had said. It was not physical strength that was required, but spiritual strength. She was right; he knew that. She would not have said it otherwise. He would follow her advice.

As if shaking off his desire for food, he got quietly to his feet. First he hunched the muscles of his shoulders and then released them. Next he lifted each leg in turn slightly off the floor and straightened it out. He let his body relax, and inhaled deeply. Letting out the breath slowly, he put his cloak on his saddle and turned to the fire. It was burning low, so he put on some more wood, watching the pieces steam and hiss as their dampness rolled away. After checking the stones around the fire, to assure himself that they would keep it safely contained, he picked up his cloak. He was ready for sleep now.

Suddenly he was overtaken again by hunger. This time the pang was sharper. It was as if someone were turning a hot blade in his stomach. He felt that he would be able to grasp it if he put his hand on his abdomen. Moving his head, he glanced at Mary. She was sleeping. By the light of the fire, he could see the peaceful rise and fall of her shoulder under her cloak. He knew that he should not eat. It would be better not to. But surely a little food could not cause any harm? He was only thinking the words, but it was as if they were being spoken into his ear by someone. He almost looked round, but he glanced again at Mary. She was still asleep. He stepped to his bag and felt inside it, carefully trying to make no noise. His fingers touched a piece of bread. Pulling it out, he began to nibble at it. Mary stirred and a sound came from between her lips. He gave a start. Nervously he looked at her, but she had not awoken. He moved his gaze back to the piece of bread in his hand. His hunger was no longer there. Quietly he replaced the bread in his bag and picked up his cloak. He put the bag down near to the one which Mary was using as a pillow and, after wrapping his cloak round him, he lay down with his head almost touching that of his still-sleeping companion.

He was soon asleep. Eventually, a dream came. He was in a room with smooth walls of a stone that shone like polished steel. There was no door. Nor could a ceiling be seen. Even though he tried to climb out, there seemed to be no way to do so.

In his small cave out on the moor, James was fighting against a sleepiness that was creeping through his muscles like a sly syrup. He had been coping well with the witch. She had been silent for some time and he had seen little movement inside the circle of flame. He began to think enviously about Carlyon and how he had probably found lodgings and was even then no doubt eating a meal. Then an almost overpowering urge to sleep came upon him. He shook himself and fought against it. Stretching up his arms to touch the underside of the rock beneath which he was sheltering, he tried to exercise wakefulness into his body. He could not understand why he was feeling so sleepy. Perhaps if he was to eat something? That might be the answer. But it seemed to be too much trouble to reach into his bag. Forcing open his eyes, he saw that it was time to raise the fire again. He took up the flint, but a tugging lethargy clogged his fingers and he was unable to strike it. Before he knew it, he was in a deep sleep.

The fire died down and the witch, who had been lying on the ground, raised her head. Slowly she got to her feet as her strength returned. At last she stepped triumphantly over what was left of the flames and looked malevolently across at the small cave in which James was sleeping. The muscles of her drawn face moved to pull her lips into a wicked smile. Walking over to James, she gazed down at him for some seconds. He slept on regardless. The witch lifted up a small stick which she was holding in her left hand. She moved to strike him, but paused. Instead, she struck the rock that was protecting him. Angrily fixing her features into a foul grimace, she tugged her cloak about her and set off across the moor through the night in the direction taken by Carlyon and Mary.

# 13

When Carlyon woke up in the tiny cottage where he and Mary had spent a night, the fire was nothing but cold ashes and there was a strange plopping noise. As he pulled his knees up towards his chest in an attempt to shake away the coldness that was pinching at him, he realised that the noise was being caused by melting snow dripping off what was left of the cottage's roof. He lifted his head to look round. It was dawn, but because the sky was packed with heavy cloud, there was very little light. There was enough to see his belongings, though, and, when he turned his head farther, Mary. In the night she had moved to lie beside him. Or had he moved to lie beside her? He couldn't remember. Either way, they had kept each other warm. He pulled himself into a sitting position, and the movement woke Mary. Instantly awareness took her and she climbed straight to her feet.

Pulling her cloak round her and shivering slightly, she said, "Ah! It's morning."

"Yes." He got slowly to his feet. "I'll start the fire and we'll have some breakfast. Then we must be on our way immediately."

While he was striking his flint for the fire, Mary yawned and ran her fingers through her hair to straighten it. Then, as if she had shaken herself, she bent quickly to take a pot from one of the pouches. She filled it with water which Carlyon had brought in the night before, and put it down near the fire, which was starting to take hold. Then she went outside. By the time she returned, the fire was burning well and Carlyon was trying to balance the pot over the flames. He turned his head at the sound of her entrance, and she smiled at him.

"I'll do that," she said. "I'll make us some gruel. It won't take long."

He nodded his acceptance, knowing that she would be more capable at it than he was, and went off to the privy. When he got to the side of the house, there was enough light for him to see a set of footprints in the slushy snow going round the privy towards the back of the cottage. At first he wondered why Mary had gone there, but when he looked, he saw that the shallow depressions were already filled with water and the sides had lost their sharpness. It seemed strange that the thaw had had such a swift effect. He glanced back at his own footprints and saw Mary's mixed in with his. They were still fresh. Thoughtfully, he looked around, but there was nothing to see. Perhaps Mary had gone out in the night. He would ask her.

When he went back into the cottage, he was feeling fresher, having gathered up some of the soft snow to sluice his face. Mary had boiled up some gruel and was awaiting his return to serve it out. The aroma of the oatmeal caught at his nostrils, bringing back his hunger. He had forgotten that he had not eaten for many hours. Cupping his hands round the wooden bowl she gave him, he said a simple grace and took a mouthful. Mary watched him, as if wanting to know if he liked it. Then she lifted up her own bowl. After she had taken a mouthful, she lowered the bowl and looked at it with puzzlement on her face.

"Is something amiss?" he asked.

"There seems to be a flavour I don't know. Perhaps it's the water."

"I would think so. The taste is excellent to me. Eat up, we must be leaving."

They continued to eat, and Carlyon remembered the footprints, but before he could mention them, he suddenly found it difficult to lift the bowl to his lips. Lethargy was holding down his arms, preventing him from eating any more. He saw that Mary seemed to be feeling the same. She looked at him, and as if from far away he heard her speak, bringing out each word slowly and carefully.

"Something is wrong. I fear magic. Somehow the witch has done something."

This meant nothing to Carlyon. The witch was miles away, being held by James. He was just tired. He had eaten enough. If they began to move, they would soon regain their energy. Taking a breath, he let his bowl drop to the floor and then pushed at his saddle to get himself to his feet. There was no strength in his arms. He was unable to move from where he was. It came to him that he had not fasted the previous evening, as Mary had advised. It made him wonder if his spiritual weakness was causing his physical tiredness. He thought to ask Mary, but shame held his tongue still. He would try again to get to his feet, but when he looked up, his heart jolted in his breast, almost causing movement in the rest of his body that had hitherto been impossible. The witch was standing before him.

"I've caught up with you at last," she scowled. "A merry dance you've led me, but you were foolish to think you could escape. I came here while you were sleeping and I placed a potion in your water. You are now in my power."

"Have you given us poison?" Carlyon managed to ask.

"Not at all. The potion has merely held you for me. It will soon wear off. I wish you no harm, despite all the trouble you've caused me. I only want my sword. If you give it to me, I'll go away and leave you in peace."

Before he could answer, he heard Mary say, "She's lying to get what she wants. Don't give her the sword, whatever she says."

"Take no notice of that peasant wench, Sir Knight. You and I are of gentle birth. We will deal with each other as gentlefolk. Give me the sword and I shall leave. On that I pledge you my word."

"No! The sword is mine and I'll never give it up. Do your worst."

"My worst? You've never seen the like of that. You will do what I say." She looked about her, sticking her head out on her neck like a crow as she checked that she had missed nothing in her earlier search. "Where is the sword?"

"Never!"

Carlyon was able to move his limbs only with difficulty, but he recalled that the witch had said that the potion would soon wear off. He just had to hold on. She was looking at him with fury sparking out of her eyes. He was almost pushed back by the malevolence of it, but he held her gaze.

"You won't win," she hissed. "You think you'll be able to do something when my potion wears off? Hah! You haven't seen my powers. That boy you left to try to hold me has seen something of them."

"James? What have you done with him, you foul creature? Say now!"

"I don't have to say anything," she said, and cackled in cruel amusement. "You should not have left a boy to do such a task."

"A boy he may be, but he has a man's heart. Where is he?"

"Why should I care? He was your squire," she said nonchalantly, as if determined to twist a spike into Carlyon's heart. "He is where I left him, mayhap. It may be he breathes yet. Until I get the sword, you'll never know."

Carlyon's body was racked with a silent groan that even the lethargy brought on by the witch's potion could not prevent. He was shaken by the feeling that he was responsible for James's death. His squire had died alone, and because his master had failed him. Was a sword, was any artefact, worth the loss of a human life? Perhaps he should give up the sword and trust the witch to keep her side of the bargain. But he had no time to make a decision on that. While his angry and unhappy mind was shaking with those thoughts, the witch spoke again. This time, there was a calmness to her tone that seemed even more chilling than her fury.

"There is time. You won't be able to hold out against me. You'll do what I say."

She said no more, to Carlyon's surprise. She stood there looking at him appraisingly and his skin seemed to ripple under her gaze. He waited in fear of what she would do to him, and prayed that he would find the strength to hold out against her. When she did move, he could not prevent himself from flinching, but she was not moving towards him. She stepped over and took hold of Mary's sluggish arm. With a rough tug that seemed also to jerk Carlyon's body, she pulled the hapless damsel to her feet. Half-carrying and half-pulling, the witch took Mary out of the cottage. Carlyon watched her go. He was willing his leaden limbs to move, but as if chained to the spot, he was held motionless.

He was unsure how long the witch was away. It could not have been long, because the fire was still burning when she returned. He noticed that even as he struggled again in vain to get to his feet to confront her. She cackled at his efforts, as if they amused her. His continuing impotence seemed to be putting her into a good mood.

"Struggle, struggle, Sir Knight. It'll avail you nothing. I care not."

"You misbegotten hag! Where's Mary? What have you done with her?"

"What have you done with the sword? I've taken your wench to a secret place, and there she'll stay until I release her. Her freedom, her life – all in your hands, good sir."

Carlyon sank back on his saddle. He accepted that there was no point in struggling. For an instant, fear flowed through him – but for Mary, not for himself. He felt responsible for her plight. He was sure that it was his carelessness – his arrogance, even – that had put her in such danger. Perhaps he should give up the sword in exchange for her safe return? But Mary herself had told him not to give it up, whatever happened. Should he disobey her this time? How would he know that the witch would indeed bring Mary back? No. He would wait and watch. His strength was sure to return and he would fight the witch or die in the attempt.

The witch seemed not to be in a hurry. While he had been sitting and agonising, she had been flitting about the room, peering and prying here and there. She was almost ignoring Carlyon, as if sure that she was in control. At last she looked at him. "I wish to play before I leave," she said. "I'll teach you a lesson, because of

155

all the trouble you've caused me. You think you've suffered? You'll serve me for a while this morning." She poured a little water into a small cup. From her bag she took a phial. Taking out the stopper, she tipped three drops into the water, then carefully she shook the cup to disperse the colourless liquid. Then she held it to Carlyon's lips. "Drink this. You'll be able to move again."

He thought to refuse. He was fearful of what the witch was giving him, so he held his lips closely together and tried to move his head away. It was in vain. His muscles were still not his own. The witch easily pushed his mouth open enough to get the lip of the cup inside. Her new potion was drunk. He spluttered as it went down his throat, but within seconds he began to feel a pricking in his arms and legs, as if blood were rushing through his veins once more after being long pent up. He jumped to his feet, and stamped and shook until he felt easier. He looked round at the witch, who was watching him with a sardonic smile on her lips. She held up a finger.

"Softly, Sir Knight. You are still in my power. I can kill or I can allow to live, as I will. You will do what I say. Then I will take the sword."

She turned her back on him and began to search inside her bag. Carlyon started to lift his arms in front of him with his fingers curled, ready to grab. He could take her round the throat and squeeze the life out of her. But he stayed where he was. She had shown that she had powers beyond his physical ones. She had made him weak; then she had restored his strength. It was impossible to know what else she could do. And he could not kill her without first finding out what had happened to Mary and James. At the least, he could see that they were given a Christian burial. He lowered his hands to his sides and resolved to obey the witch meekly, until a chance should arise for him to gain the upper hand. He must be cautious. She turned and looked at him, as if trying to guess what he was thinking. He lowered his head slightly, so that she could not see into his eyes.

"So be it," she muttered, seemingly to herself. Then, more loudly, "Here! Take these. I want you to cook me a stew."

He saw that she had in her hands a piece of salt pork and some vegetables – cabbage leaves, a leek and a turnip. "I know nought of kitchen work," he protested weakly. "I don't cook."

"You'll learn now, before I leave. I'll have you sweep out this place also. You'll be my servant now, until I tire of you." She looked at him and then added slyly, "Make a good job of the stew and I'll bring your maiden to share it. Refuse to obey me and she will die. Go to it! I must rest now after travelling all night." In her confidence, she went to a corner of the room and lay down, wrapping her cloak around her.

Carlyon stood, holding the pork and the vegetables, and watched. Fury at her arrogance burned through him like a flame and made him tremble, so that he lost his grip on the turnip. The dull thud of it hitting the floor broke his trance. Shaking himself, he knelt down and spread out what he was holding in front of him. He had no idea how to cook a stew, except that he thought that water would be needed. He also felt that the meat ought to be cut into smaller pieces. If only Mary were there to do it for him. Looking round, he saw a flat stone near the fire. He blew off the dust, wiped it with his sleeve, and laid the meat on top. As he took out his knife to cut the pork, he glanced over at the witch. Her body was moving rhythmically, and to his relief he saw that she had fallen asleep. He looked down at his knife. It would be a simple matter to slit her throat. But suppose she was protected by magic? And he still did not know where Mary was, or how to release her if she was held by magic. Reluctantly, he bent his head and coarsely cut the witch's pork into pieces. Looking at the vegetables, he thought that they also should be chopped. He wished now that he had watched more closely when Mary had made a stew in Thomas's cottage. It was difficult to know if he was doing it correctly. After he had sliced up the turnip, he wondered if he should have wiped off the bits of earth on its skin, but it was too late for that. Perhaps soil was vaporised in the cooking and disappeared in the steam? He didn't know. He looked at the witch again. She was still sleeping. It would be good to have the stew ready when she awoke. After resting she might be in a good mood and so tell him where Mary was. He quickly put more wood on the fire and picked up the pot in which Mary had made the gruel. Momentarily he seemed to feel her presence, encouraging him, but then it was gone. He wished that she were with him to help. She always seemed to know what to do.

Gathering himself, he looked for water. There was none. He glanced nervously at the sleeping witch and went outside with the pot. By the door, he looked about him. Through the trees he saw what looked like a pond, and walked over to it. Although most of the snow had melted, there was still ice on the pond, but he broke it easily with his boot heel at the edge. After filling the pot, he returned to the cottage, but before going in, he decided to check that the sword was still well hidden. It was undisturbed. No one would know that it was there, unless told. He nodded his satisfaction, and put down his pot of water so that he could look over the horses. They seemed content. There was water in the trough, and he picked up his pot to go back into the cottage. There he first went over to his bags, meaning to take out some oats for the horses. He unbuckled a bag with haste, anxious to return to making the stew, but was interrupted. His shield, which was leaning against a bag, spoke quietly but clearly to him.

"Do not work so quickly."

Carlyon gave a start and looked at the boss, which had become a face again. So much had been happening that he had forgotten about the shield. "I have to be quick. The sooner I make the stew, the sooner the witch will release Mary."

"She will do nothing until she has the sword."

"Then I shall have to give her the sword. I must save Mary."

"That will not save her. Nor you. As soon as she has the sword, she will kill both you and Mary."

Disappointment pulsed through Carlyon like a pendulum and he almost swayed. He had been trying to convince himself that things would come out right, but he had suspected that the witch could not be trusted. "What can I do?" he asked, the words coming out like a moan.

"You must work more slowly and wait until James comes to help you."

"James? Is he alive? Is he safe?"

"He is alive. He fell asleep, because you did not fast last night. Give him time to get to you."

Carlyon, angry with himself for his weakness the previous evening, but hopeful that all was not yet lost, took some food out for the horses. Then he quietly returned. The witch was still as he had left her. A sharp noise, as a stick in the fire cracked, made him jump, but it did not disturb the witch. He went over to the fire. For a few seconds he looked, then, reaching carefully with a gloved hand, he pulled out some of the brands, so that the fire was not burning so cheerfully. Taking his time, he put into the pot the meat and vegetables that he had chopped. With his hands he ripped apart the cabbage leaves and added them. Having done that, he leaned back on his haunches and looked around thoughtfully. There was nothing else to prepare. He sighed and placed the pot over the fire on the balancing stones at either side. When it was steady, he picked up Mary's stirring stick and gave the mixture a tentative poke. After that, mindful of what the witch had said, he began to wander about the room, making desultory attempts to tidy it. Occasionally he returned to the fire and gave the pot a stir, as he felt that that was the sort of thing that cooks did.

The water was not yet boiling when the witch woke up. She stretched her limbs like an uncurling cat and then carelessly got to her feet. Shaking down her gown, she put her cloak back over her shoulders and came across to look at the stew. Instantly, her mood changed. "What's this?" she snapped. "Not even boiling yet. Build the fire higher, you knave. I'm getting hungry. If that's not ready soon, I'll have to eat something else – a young wench's heart, mayhap?"

Her anger seemed to be coming out of her mouth like flames that scorched Carlyon. He jumped to his feet and tried to placate her. "I'm sorry, my lady, truly I am. I'm not an expert in this sort of thing. I'll have it ready directly, I assure you. Please do nought to harm."

"Pah!" As if it was not worth saying anything more to him, the witch abruptly swept her cloak around her, turned, and strode out of the cottage.

Carlyon watched the doorway anxiously, thinking that she would return. After a few seconds he realised that he had better look busy, in case she did. He picked up some pieces of wood and poked them into the fire. Worry at the situation made him use more force than he meant to, and sparks flew out. Jerkily he moved to the other side and used a piece of wood to gather the burning brands together and arrange the fire carefully, so that heat was directed at the pot of stew. There was nothing else that he could do, except watch the pot and wonder where Mary had been hidden.

His musings were interrupted by the sonorous voice of the shield, which came softly into his ear from across the room. "Mary is still safe. I know not where she lies, but I can feel her heart beating and hear her breath. Have faith and hold on. It is a long journey. I cannot see the ending."

"I'm trying," said Carlyon unhappily, as he got up from his haunches and stepped over to the shield, "but the witch is so powerful. I don't seem able to fight her."

"Remain steadfast. She is not all-powerful. Even now she is trying to find where you have hidden the sword. All of her wicked powers are of no help to her in that."

"Suppose she does find the sword. Will she leave us in peace then?"

"If she should find the sword, then she will be able to commit more evil than you can imagine. But time is passing. You must keep delaying the witch until James arrives. Then he will help you to defeat her."

"How will we do that? How can she be killed?"

"There is a certain way, and you must do it exactly as I tell you. First she must be set on fire."

"How will I do that?"

"You will use the flint which James will bring. No other flint will work. When the witch has been burned, you must stab her with your sword. When you have done that, she must be drowned. Only then will she die. She knows that. She will offer to release Mary in order to prevent it."

The shield now fell silent. Carlyon looked at it for a few seconds, then returned to the fire. Sitting on his saddle, he watched the pot and occasionally gave it a stir or built up the fire again. From time to time, as he thought over what lay ahead of him, his fists clenched involuntarily and his body tensed, as if about to leap up. For all of the shield's optimism, he felt that there was danger hovering around the cottage.

It was almost midday when the witch returned. She said nothing and went to peer into the pot. Giving it a stir with the stick, she grunted her satisfaction. "Serve it out," she snapped. "That'll do now."

"I think it needs a little longer. To be tender."

"I can't wait. Serve it out!" She sat down on his saddle and looked at him with eyes that had narrowed in their ferocity.

He licked his lips nervously, but did not flinch. He tried to play for more time. "Where's Mary?" he asked firmly. "You said she would join us."

This time the witch laughed, boldly and callously. "I've changed my mind. I've carried the wench to another place to keep her as safe as you seem to be keeping my sword. When you give up the sword, I'll tell you where she is. Serve out my stew!"

She lifted her arm, as if about to curse him. He realised that he could delay no longer, and he picked up a bowl.

# 14

After Carlyon had served out a bowl of stew for the witch, he stood and watched helplessly as she raised it to her mouth. However, it was too hot and she lowered it again.

"Don't stand there looking at me," she scowled. "Go and bring the sword."

He hesitated momentarily, looking fully into her face. Then he turned and left the cottage.

Outside, he found that the thaw had continued. There was very little snow left. He saw the witch's footprints trailing away through the trees, but they petered out when he tried to follow them. There was an occasional depression in the mud that might have been caused by a foot, but although he continued in the same direction for a while, he had to admit defeat. He stood where he was at the edge of the copse and looked in front of him, wondering if Mary lay in that direction, or whether the witch had turned off. She must be along there somewhere, he told himself. There's no path here. He had seen that the witch's traces led through the trees in a more-or-less straight line, and it was reasonable to assume that she had continued in the same way across the heath that lay in front of him. Raising his head, he stood and stared, but there was no movement; nothing to suggest that anything was hidden there. If Mary *was* on the heath, he could perhaps search for days without finding her. And if the witch had taken her over the heath and beyond, then he would not know where to look. No! He had to get the witch to tell him. He would force her to do so, when he was killing her. If death came to frighten her, she would surely tell him, in order to save her life.

Abruptly, anger at his impotence turned his body round as if on a spinning shield, and he strode purposefully back towards the cottage. There he glanced at the place where he had hidden the sword. It seemed to be undisturbed and there was still no sign that there was anything there. For some seconds he looked at his horses, seemingly content as they watched him. He had no idea what to do next, and they gave him no inspiration.

Suddenly he heard the sound of hooves on the roadway. A horse was approaching at a steady gallop. He hurried over to stand by the road. This was the first sign of humanity other than himself, Mary and the witch that he had seen that day. He watched curiously as the horse and rider drew closer, and then his heart seemed to bounce into his throat as he recognised James. Joy pushed him out into the road and he waved his arms as a signal. At last, he thought that there was hope.

James was almost upon Carlyon before he began to rein in his horse; he seemed so desperate to reach him as soon as possible. As he slowed, first to a trot and then almost immediately to a stop, Carlyon stepped up to hold the bridle of the excited horse, which was tossing its head and blowing heavily. He was still trying to calm the horse when James jumped off. Letting the horse go, Carlyon embraced his squire, relief at his safety almost driving his other problems from his mind.

"Thank the Lord, you're safe," he cried. "I feared me I wouldn't see you again."

"Oh, sire, I failed you. I let the witch escape. I fell asleep. I'm so sorry. I don't know how it happened."

Carlyon, who knew how it had happened, brushed aside his young squire's apology and tried to relieve his obvious devastation. "Have no worry, James. You did well, holding the witch as you did. And you're here in good time to help again."

"Where did the witch go? Has she come here? Has Mary been able to keep her away?"

Carlyon's face set in hard lines around his mouth and eyes and he stepped away from James. He took hold again of the horse's bridle, as if for support, and told him how the witch had caught them unawares and taken Mary away to a secret hiding place.

"Oh, sire, it was all my fault. What can we do?"

"There's no blame for you. The fault was mine," Carlyon admitted, and then hurried on before James could catch up on that. "The witch is in yonder cottage. Unsaddle your horse and rest him down. Hobble him over there, out of sight. The witch knows not you're here, so we can surprise her."

When James had unsaddled his horse and put a blanket over its trembling back, he returned to Carlyon, who was thoughtfully considering the pond.

"We have to make the witch tell us where Mary is," Carlyon said.

"Can't we hold her with fire from the flint until she tells us?"

"I don't know if she will. She'll only tell us if she's afraid of dying."

"How can we do that? She's protected by powerful magic."

"I know how to kill her. She has to be burned by fire from your flint. Then I must stab her with my sword. Finally, she must be drowned. This pond here will be deep enough. We have to entice her out." Carlyon looked around, and then it came to him. "You can put on my armour, so that you look like me. I'll hide behind yon juniper bush. If you stand by the water's edge, you can strike your flint against her and I can creep out and stab her. We'll tell her that we'll throw her into the pond if she doesn't tell us where Mary is. She'll think that she can save her life, but I don't need to keep my word to a witch."

"You can rely on me, sire," James said fervently. "I won't let you down this time."

Carlyon hid his embarrassment by quickly embracing his squire. He then led him quietly to where Champion and the packhorse were waiting patiently. Moving quickly but quietly, he took off his overtunic and surcoat and exchanged them with James.

As he was opening his pouch to get at his armour, James asked him, "Do I need to put on the full suit? I might have to move quickly."

"I'm not sure. We'll see. I have to make certain that she can't tell who you are, so she's no reason to think you're not I."

James nodded and pulled on Carlyon's mail shirt, and then stood while Carlyon strapped the steel breastplate round him. Once the surcoat had been put on, Carlyon stood back and looked critically at his squire. His frame was rather gawky compared with Carlyon's, but by tightening the belt to pull in the surcoat, it looked better.

"Yes, that may do. I think we need not put the plate on your arms and legs. It won't fit properly. Quickly, now. Time is passing. Put on the hood and my helmet."

James covered his head with a mail hood and then, without bothering to settle it tidily round his shoulders, put on the helmet. Even with the visor up, it was impossible to tell who it was.

"That'll do," said Carlyon. "Do you have the flint?"

"Yes, here it is."

"Good. Go and stand you by the pond near the juniper. I'll call out the witch and, God willing, we'll put an end to her evil."

James murmured his agreement and moved away. Carlyon went over to where he had hidden the sword. Relief that it was still there was a warm surge through his chest, even though he knew of no reason why it would not be waiting for him. He pulled it free from the thatch, making more noise than he expected in his haste, but it seemed louder in his imagination than in actual fact. At least the witch gave no sign of having heard it. He pulled the sword out of its scabbard to look at it. Despite the overcast grey sky, the blade had a shimmering brightness that was almost humming. He put it back in its scabbard and buckled it round his waist. Taking a deep breath, he prepared for the next part of his plan. Quietly as he could, he went round to the doorway of the cottage and peered in. The witch was sitting on his saddle with her back to him. She was still eating, having taken a second helping of the stew. Possibly Carlyon had proved to be a better cook than he had feared. He smiled grimly and stepped back a few feet.

"Lady!" he called. "Lady! If you want the sword now, I have it for you by the pond."

Without waiting to see what effect his words had, he ran the few yards through the trees to the pond. James was already there by the juniper. He was standing with his back three quarters on to the cottage, so that the flint in his hand could not be seen. Carlyon hissed to him to stand firm and went to crouch behind the bush. Carefully, he drew the sword. Its haft nestled in his hand, and suddenly confidence seemed to flow through into his arm and straight to his heart.

The witch was soon there. She was so eager that she had not even wiped her mouth and chin: Carlyon could plainly see the dribble. Nor had she put on her cloak, as if she could not feel the cold. She was speaking as she approached. "Where's the sword? At last! Where is it?"

James did not speak. He had turned his head, so that he could see her through the helmet's eye slit. His hands were hidden and he waited until she was near enough to touch.

"Where is it? Hand it over!"

Carlyon, in his hiding place, was worried by a note of suspicion that he could hear in the witch's peremptory tone. Perhaps she was wondering why James was not holding the sword in his hand, and suspected a trick. Carlyon tensed in readiness, willing James to strike the flint. Now! Do it now! his anxious soul urged James. If he did not move soon, the witch would suspect a trick and it would be too late.

At last James moved. He still said nothing, but he twisted his body to face the witch and brought out his hands from behind his back. He almost fumbled, but his strike was successful: a flame leaped out to enfold the witch and she began to burn. Yet to Carlyon's horror, she was not actually consumed. The flames flickered over her body and she was held by them – her arms raised, as if to protect her face – but her clothes and her flesh seemed untouched. He had to act quickly, before the flames died down. He

168

dashed out from his hiding place and almost faltered as the witch turned towards him. She was looking directly at him, but as if his sword had a mind of its own, it raised his arm. The blade plunged into the witch's chest and emerged from her back. Carlyon knew that it had gone through her heart. As he withdrew the sword, she sank to her knees, fury twisting her face into a terrifying mask. He watched, preparing to strike again if she threatened anything, but she rolled over onto her back. Now she could be tossed into the pond, but first Carlyon had to make her tell him where Mary was.

"Your life is in my hands now, wicked one. Tell me where you've hidden the damsel Mary, or I shall throw you into the pond and drown you."

The witch looked at him with hatred filling her eyes like burning tears. She seemed to be trying to summon up her powers. Carlyon tensed, but only words came out of her mouth.

"You think you've got the best of me. I know you'll kill me."

"No, no, I won't! I'll spare your life, if you only tell me what you've done with Mary."

"That's not so. If you don't kill me now, then I'll kill you. I know that is what will happen. I'll never tell you where the wench is hidden. I've taken her from you and I would not have returned her even if you had given me the sword. She's imprisoned in an underground cavern, locked in a stone coffin that no human hand can open." The witch had been gasping out her words with difficulty. The flames had died, but still she seemed unable to move. Now she looked at the sword in Carlyon's hand and laughed. It was as if she no longer cared what might happen to her.

Anger at her callous laughter surged through Carlyon's head and flashed like a bright light in front of his eyes, blinding him momentarily. Riven by a thought that he would never see Mary again, he cried out, "Then you will die! You'll harm no other of God's creatures. Go down to Hell, where you belong. James! Help me!"

Carlyon took hold of an arm and a leg and James quickly jumped to take her other side. Between them they swung her out and threw her into the pond, cracking the brittle ice.

"Die, you foul and evil creature!" Making an effort to recover his balance, Carlyon watched through eyes that had unexpectedly filled with tears. Then fright seized him as he saw that the witch was floating on the water. She was not drowning.

James saw it too. "She's not sinking! Her gown is keeping her up. We need a stick to push her down."

They looked around, but there was nothing suitable. Carlyon ran to a tree, thinking that he might be able to break off a branch. He was pulling fruitlessly at a leafless oak when he heard a splashing from the pond. Fearing the worst, he looked round frantically. However, it was James. He was wading into the water.

"I'll make her sink," James cried. "I know what to do."

By the time that Carlyon had run back to the pond and begun to wade into the chilly water, James had thrown his full length onto the witch. The weight of Carlyon's armour was taking the two of them down.

"She's sinking!" he shouted, the words sounding muffled. "I can do it now, sire. You go and look for Mary. I'll join you soon, when I'm sure the witch is dead."

Carlyon hesitated, then saw that the witch was now beneath the water. James was pressing her down. He turned and left the pond. Looking back, he saw that James himself was partially submerged. The witch could not be seen, but was evidently not struggling. Carlyon hurried through the copse and out onto the heath. Back and forth he cast, erratically at first, but then trying to cover the area systematically. Perhaps for an hour he walked about, until he thought that it would be easier if James would help. It was then that he realised that time had been passing, but James had not joined him. His breath hot in his breast, anxiety drove his legs back to the pond.

He saw James's horse still hobbled amongst the trees, but when he reached the pond, shock halted his steps. There was no sign of movement on the water. Only the churned mud on the bank where Carlyon and James had burned and stabbed the witch, and the broken ice, showed that anything had happened. There was not even the sound of a sighing breeze. Carlyon approached the water's edge and looked out. A horrible fear that something had happened to James made him lift an arm helplessly, as if to reach out. He waded into the water up to his knees and peered down, but it was too murky to see anything at all. He waded deeper and bent to feel with his hands. It was hopeless. Even when he waded in up to his waist and could reach out to touch the unbroken ice, he felt nothing on the bottom of the pond but cold, clinging mud. For almost a minute he thrashed about, and then the cold began to numb and cramp the muscles of his legs. He knew that he had to leave the pond.

Struggling to the side, he fell to his knees, as if a millstone of hopelessness had rolled onto him. His heart cried for James, who had given his life in his master's service. He groaned and wondered if it had been worth it. Getting to his feet, he stumbled round the edge of the pond, driven by the hope that he would find James somewhere in the trees. There was no trace of him. Finally he stopped and leaned despairingly against a tree. Then suddenly he began to shiver. Cold crept up through his body, clawing along his flesh with icy hands. Unable to control his trembling, he knew that he had to move. Trying to walk quickly, he went to the cottage. It was empty. James had not returned there. However, seeing that there were still embers in the fire, he blew them into life. Fighting to control his shivering, he put on the few pieces of wood that were left and took off his wet hose and breeches.

Later, after changing and getting warmth back into his body, he squatted by the dying fire and pondered his next move. He would try to find Mary, if she was still alive. If he went in the direction that the witch seemed to have gone during her absence while he was making the stew, then surely he would come across a sign of some kind. He must do all he could to find Mary. She was a peasant woman, but he had grown to believe that she was the equal of any lady in the land. As he sat there, he remembered the thoughtful way in which she moved while doing her little tasks. He remembered the lilt of her voice; her accent so different from his. Tears came to his eyes at the thought that she might be lost to him. A spasm of unusual longing seemed to shake him, as if a flame had licked out from the fire. He had never felt like that about Lady Patrina.

The sudden remembrance of Patrina almost gave his body a physical jerk. He was reminded that he had made a vow that had to be kept. His task had to be completed. He must win his lady and defeat his rival. He got to his feet and looked around the deserted room, remembering, despite himself, how he and Mary had lain together by the fire during the night. Giving his head a shake of irritated acceptance, he left the cottage. There was no longer anything there for him. Even the memories would only pain him.

He led the horses through the trees and mounted Champion once they were out on the heath. At first he rode slowly in a straight line, occasionally standing in the stirrups to look around, seeking something that might strike him. He refused to admit that his search was hopeless, even though he had no idea what he was looking for. After a while he began to cast about, looking for tracks in any area of soft ground or any remaining patches of snow. There was nothing to help him. In the end he had to accept that the witch could have gone in any direction once she was on the heath. His task was hopeless. Mary was lost to him forever.

# 15

*C*arlyon continued to wander to and fro across the heath until it was too dark for him to see. For a while he even groped miserably about in the dark, hoping that the moon would rise, but it was too cloudy and at last he had to stop. By then he had no idea where he was. Occasionally during the afternoon he had seen sheep and guessed that a hamlet of some kind was not too far away, but he had little hope of finding it in the darkness. He had left it too late. At least he seemed, from what he could tell, to have stumbled upon a sheltered spot in a hollow. He would make the best of it and spend the night there.

The night was not a comfortable one. He awoke several times, either from cold or from some other discomfort. It was a relief when dawn began to scrape its fingering streaks across the sky and he could climb out of his cloak to stretch his limbs. It took a minute or two before fluidity returned and his stiffness no longer hindered him. Gratefully he looked around and broke off some branches from a bush to make a fire. Unfortunately his kindling was too damp and he had to abandon his efforts. Disgustedly kicking the small heap of wood which he had made, he angrily pulled his cloak around him and went to unhobble the horses.

As he saddled Champion, the increasing daylight had no effect on his misery. He was alone, wearing a squire's simple clothes, and unsure what he should do or which way to go. When all was ready, he held Champion's bridle and looked at the horse, which was looking placidly back at him.

"What'll we do, Champion? It's all gone amiss. The soft south wind I hoped for has been nought but a bitter north. I fear I'm making a thicket for myself that I can't get through. I should never have agreed to come on this chase after wild birds. What point does it have? I'm alone and lost, alone and lost. But no. No. I've built my own thicket. Surely I can find the power to cut through it? I must finish what I set out to do. What else can I do? I've come this far. I will continue."

He was looking at his horse, but his eyes were not registering, as his mind had wandered off into the wilderness. He seemed to be muttering more to himself than to Champion. Suddenly Champion snickered and the sound seemed to strike Carlyon's body like green vitriol. He straightened up and looked firmly at the horse. Nodding as if in agreement with something that Champion had said, he set his face.

"I must keep my vow. There's nothing left but that. At least I can achieve that. I can find the flowers of the swan, take them back, and claim Lady Patrina. She is awaiting me. I must lose no more time, or Sir John will prevail."

Champion's head moved to look at him and he stamped his forelegs in the cold, as if eager to be on his way.

"Yes, old friend. It's only you and I now. If there are still dangers ahead, then we'll have to face them together."

Fired now with a determination that had coated his backbone in steel, Carlyon mounted Champion and set off out of the hollow in which he had spent the night. In the open, he moved in what he judged from the light in the sky to be a southerly direction. Soon he came upon a track, and as this seemed to lead him in almost the same direction, he followed it. Before long, he came upon a small monastery. He obtained food and sought directions. The road did indeed lead southwards, but his informant had a warning for him.

"A league and a half beyond, there's a forest. Don't take the road through the forest. There are wild birds there that attack men. There are also wild beasts that kill. Hunters have gone in there to try to take them, but none has come out alive. You must go round the forest."

"How long will that take?"

The monk shrugged and said that it would not be more than three days at that time of year. When Carlyon expressed surprise at the estimate, he was told that there were marshes and that the going would be slow and heavy. Carlyon nodded and prepared for departure. He put some of James's personal effects into his own bag and, when he set off, he left the rest of his squire's few things, together with his horse, for the use of the monastery. It did not lighten his burden of sadness, but he knew that the monks would pray for James's soul.

When he got to the forest, it did not look to be very thick or threatening to him. It was mainly deciduous and he could see some way into it between the leafless trunks. The track along which he had come forked at that spot. One fork led off along the edge of the forest, miry and narrow. The other went straight on, confidently, into the trees. Carlyon sat and listened. He could hear nothing but a few innocently calling birds. He looked to the side. The trees stretched as far as he could see. Three days. That was a long time. He pulled in his lips. It would be quicker to go through the forest, and if he met any danger, he had his sword and his good right arm. Unwilling to waste any more time thinking about it, he spurred Champion forward and went in amongst the trees.

As he travelled through the forest, his confidence grew. The going was firm underfoot, and after half an hour of uneventful travel he was becoming more sure that he had made the correct decision. He remained watchful, but there was nothing to worry him…until abruptly the pathway petered out. It was almost as if no one had ever gone any farther. He dismounted and looked through the trees. At that time of year there was very little undergrowth and he saw that he would be able to thread his way through. Pulling at Champion's rein, he continued on foot, leading the horses.

He had not gone far when his watchfulness was broken by a sudden sharp rustle, as if a heavy cloth had been shaken. He looked up in the direction of the sound. In a tree ahead of him he saw three large black birds, each the size of an eagle and with hooked beak and claws to match. Again one of the birds shook itself and he saw that they were intently watching his approach. He stopped to consider. Were these the birds of which he had been forewarned? He put his hand on his sword. That and his determined skill would be sufficient to overcome any bird, large though it may be. And yet, if all three attacked at the same time, there was no guarantee that he would be able to kill them. He could at the least be seriously injured. As he hesitated, one of the birds cocked its head and seemed to look more closely at him with its brightly jewelled eye. He glanced back at the way he had come, but there was no clear escape. The birds were preparing to attack.

He got ready to pull out his sword. He was anxious about the limited space for movement with it amongst the trees, but he had practised close-quarter work. Then he suddenly had a thought.

The holy corn, which he should have given to the swans, was still in his pouch. If he were to scatter that here for these creatures, then perhaps that would distract them. It had been blessed, so would help him. Carefully he slid his hand towards the pouch, trying not to alarm the birds by moving jerkily. Feeling with his fingers, he pulled out the cloth bag, reassured by its plumpness. Momentarily he took his eyes off the restless birds as he glanced down to undo the drawstring. Then he looked around. Next to him, no more than a touch away, was a tall ash tree with a clear space at the other side of the trunk. He stepped round it and threw out his arm to scatter the seed over as wide an area as possible.

Back at the horses, he held his sword and watched, barely breathing. It was only a second or two. One of the birds pulled itself upright and then curiously flapped down to the corn. When the other two saw it eating, they quickly followed. Partly hidden by the tree, Carlyon relaxed his grip on his sword and took hold of Champion's bridle. As silently as he could, he began to move. Gently he pulled at the bridle, hoping that the horses would make no unnecessary sound to attract the attention of the birds away from the corn.

After almost an hour he began to feel safe. The birds had not followed him. He had skirted that danger. However, the forest had changed. The leafless deciduous trunks had given way to coniferous trees. The going was a little easier, because the ground was carpeted with dead pine needles. Even so, he was still unable to ride because of the low-growing branches. At least there was some sunshine, the wind having blown the cloud away, so he was able to orient himself and maintain a roughly southerly direction.

Towards midday he stopped to rest. Silence surrounded him like an impenetrable fog. There seemed to be no life in this part of the forest. Even the breeze had dropped, and the trees were motionless, as if watchful. After a few minutes he grew nervous, although there was nothing specific to justify that. He knew that he ought to rest, but a prickly feeling urged him to start moving again and get out of the forest as soon as possible. He pushed the stopper back into the small flask of ale from which he had been drinking. Moving away from the tree against which he had been leaning, he looked ahead, hoping to see an end to the forest. He peered up at the sunlight which formed an uneven ladder through the branches. Pointlessly, he wished that he was still in the deciduous part of the forest, because there would have been more light. The low sun did little to dispel the gloom on the forest floor, merely tantalising him with its unreachable beams.

He moved to put the flask back in his bag, and then stopped. A rustling sound made him turn. Intently, he strained to tell its direction. It was ahead. Then he heard it from the side. Then from behind him. For a moment he thought that something was using magic to leap around him, but he realised that there was more than one of whatever it was. He could not see them, but he felt the hairs on the back of his head move, as if being pulled by a gentle magnet. Gripping the scabbard that was fastened to his saddle, he pulled out his sword, intending to defend himself to the utmost, whatever the terrors were. He reached for his shield, then stayed his hand. In the shadows, the boss had become a face once more.

"Stay your sword! There are too many beasts for you to overcome. You must give them fresh blood and so make your escape. You must kill the horses."

"Kill the horses? Both of them? I can't kill Champion. I won't. He's been too faithful to me."

"You must kill both. The sacrifice is required. Do it now. Time is passing. Use the sword and chop off their heads."

Carlyon looked with horror at the shield and then at the horses. It seemed to be an impossible thing that he had to do. Then the sound of movement made him lift his head. He thought it had come from immediately to his side, but when he looked, there was nothing. Then he did see something. Turning his head, he could see dark shapes moving through the trees, as if circling him. Now and then there was a flash, as from an eye. Groaning, he raised his sword, extending his upper arm straight out from the shoulder. A second he hesitated. Then he brought the blade down on the neck of the packhorse. To his surprise, the sword cut cleanly through the flesh and the bone. It was as if the weapon had under its own volition taken charge to carry out the task. Blood spurted. The head fell to the ground, and with a tremulous shudder the muscles in the body relaxed. The carcass slowly sank to the forest floor.

Carlyon had stepped back. Now he looked quickly around. The shadowy beasts seemed to have come nearer. Nervously licking his lips, he looked at Champion. The horse seemed to know what was expected of him. His eyes were closed and he had turned his head away slightly. His neck was exposed. Carlyon raised his sword and then shook his head. The arm holding the sword fell. He could not do it.

"Do it now!" he seemed to hear the shield's sonorous voice command him. "Or it will be too late."

Closing his eyes, as if anguished fingers were pressing on the lids, Carlyon raised his sword again. He opened his eyes and swung the sword round. Aiming carefully, he drew the sword's tip in a line across Champion's neck. He saw blood bubble onto the brown skin, as Champion flinched sideways. Carlyon moved quickly, trying not to pause for thought. He sheathed his sword and picked up the shield. Then, grabbing his bag from Champion's saddle, which was all that he could carry, he moved off quickly through the trees. As he went, he sensed the creatures closing in, but it seemed that it was the blood that was attracting them. He was being left alone. Again his stratagem appeared to have worked, although he was too ashamed to look back, to check.

To his relief, Carlyon found that the forest did not extend much farther. In less than twenty minutes he began to see light ahead of him as the trees began to thin out. He was moving more slowly by then; the emotional excitement that had been pumping his limbs having subsided. The weariness of his thoughts was like a web of sticky filaments holding him back, but he kept pressing on. He knew that he had to press on.

When he was clear of the forest, he found himself in a soggy, almost marshy meadow, but seeing that the ground was rising slightly in front of him, he struggled over in that direction. Soon the going got easier, and when he reached the top of the slope, he found a track. This he set off to follow, but after only a few yards it divided into three. He stopped to take stock, unsure which path to take. Perhaps it would be as well to go straight on? It would surely be as good an approach as any other. As he thought that, he thought also of Champion. He had not wanted to kill his faithful horse. Nor had he wanted to leave him to those ferocious beasts. He looked down at the shield. It was leaning, almost indolently, against the bag that he had put on the ground by his feet. The polished metal caught a faint glint from the sun, but otherwise it was featureless. Had it really told him to kill Champion?

Carlyon saw the scene again. He saw how Champion had almost seemed to be offering his neck, as if he knew what was required of him to save his master. Carlyon had not had the courage to kill him, but Champion was unlikely to have escaped. Carlyon tried not to think about what would have been the poor animal's fate. He had his own to worry about. A sly fear came into his mind that there might yet be trouble lying before him, because he had not followed the instruction to kill both horses. He remembered also that he no longer had the holy corn to placate the swans. Perhaps there would still be great misfortune yet to come.

At that point he could not prevent himself from ruefully pulling in his lips. He could not think what more misfortune could befall him than already had. He was alone, on foot, and with nothing but a small bag and ill-fitting clothes. For a few seconds he stood with his head bowed; then he shook himself. This is no time for despair, he told himself. I must carry on and finish what I started. There will surely be an end. Whatever obstacles I meet, I'll overcome them. I'm on my own now. But I'll carry on until I find what I seek – whatever it may be. As if firm hands were propelling him, he tied the shield to his bag and promptly picked it up. He put the bag over his shoulder, lifted his head to look immediately forward, and took a determined breath. Then he set off along the middle way.

On foot he made slow going. His initial eagerness was soon pulled down by his tiredness, and he began to hope for somewhere to spend the night. The countryside was wrapped gently in twilight before he found somewhere suitable. It was an empty woodman's shelter and, not knowing whether he would find anywhere habited, he went in and thankfully dropped his bag on the floor.

# 16

Carlyon awoke after a restless night and awkwardly got to his feet and walked stiffly to the door. Reaching out to the doorpost as a support, he stepped out into the sunlight. He saw no one, heard no one, when he looked around. There was only the noise of querulous rooks in the nearby trees as they prepared for their day. Slowly Carlyon went to the stream at the back of the shelter and, kneeling down, put in a hand to take up a drink of the icy water. The liquid seemed to free his muscles slightly, and he bent over farther to splash his face. This greatly refreshed him and he looked across at the other side of the stream. There were a few trees there, but he had no difficulty in seeing through their sleeveless branches. To his surprise he saw a small cottage with smoke coming out of the hole in its roof. He got to his feet and peered, wondering how he had missed it the previous afternoon. It must have been because he would have had to look directly into the sun. He glanced back at the shelter. Had he seen the cottage sooner, he would have been able to spend a more comfortable night.

He shook his head in resignation and went to the shelter for his things. As he bent to pick up his bag, his head began to swim and he almost fell over. He crouched down and took some deep breaths until he had recovered. Worriedly, he moved his head gently from side to side, wondering why he should feel so weak. He needed food. Perhaps that was all that was wrong?

Fastening on his sword, he picked up his bag and shield and went out to the stream. It was not broad – slightly more than a good stride – but when he attempted a standing jump, his legs lacked their usual power. His foot landed in the water and he was only saved from overbalancing by planting his other foot in the stream too. The water was scarcely above his ankles, but splashes went well up his legs. Irritated and jarred, but otherwise unscathed, he clambered up the shallow bank and shook each leg in turn. He glanced at the mud on his boots, but then wasted no more time.

As he approached the cottage, he was able to see that it was in a state of good repair. There was also what appeared to be a well-tended garden, although it was bare except for some frosted leeks still in the ground and some plants which he assumed to be herbs. There was also a cow, which pleased him to see and led him to hope that he might get some fresh milk. He knocked on the door.

The woman who answered his knock looked to be in her mid fifties. She was on the plump side, wearing a plain woollen gown fastened with a belt round her waist. Her greying hair was covered by an old-fashioned wimple. But it was her eyes that drew his attention the most. As blue as a clear sky, they were soft and gentle and full of a kindliness that seemed to be inviting him. Her smile of welcoming enquiry made him realise that he too was smiling for the first time in some days.

"Pray, mistress," he said, "do you have some refreshment for a traveller?"

"Of course, sir. Please to come in." She had a local accent, and her voice seemed to caress his ear like a kiss.

He stepped into her cottage and she closed the door behind him. It was simply furnished, and at first he stood on the clean and tidy floor, as if unsure what to do.

The woman seemed to guess what he wanted. "Come and sit by the fire, sir. I have some porridge and some bread."

She bustled over and pulled the simple wooden chair nearer to the fire for him to sit on it. That he did thankfully. In the peace of the cottage his head was swimming and her voice seemed to be coming from far away.

"Take off your boots. I have some warm cloths to wrap your feet. They'll soon be dry and warm."

He bent without a word to do as he was bidden, and by the time that he was unshod, his head had cleared. She herself knelt down to wrap his feet for him, and he sighed his grateful thanks. When she got to her feet, she went to a cupboard to get out a bowl.

"Where are you bound for, sir?" she asked, while ladling out porridge from a small pot on the fire.

"I'm on my way to the Wirral, but I was benighted on the road yonder. I've had a long journey."

She handed him the bowl, and after thanking her he bowed his head to say a few words of grace. When he lifted his head again, he saw that she was looking at him with a kindly, almost motherly expression. He knew he was safe with her.

"My name is Sir Carlyon de Bernedeslaw," he said, and, noticing the surprise flickering in her eyes that a knight should be on foot in such a condition, he went on. "I've gone astray in my journey. Misfortune has taken my companions, my horse and my possessions, but I thank God I've been brought here to rest awhile."

"You may rest as long as you wish, sir. My name is May and all I have is at your service."

He smiled his thanks and gratefully began to eat. May, as if in satisfaction, clapped her hands lightly together before rubbing the fingers of her left hand against the palm of her right. Then she cut him some bread and heated up some milk for him. As he ate, he watched her unfussy and competent movements. There was something familiar about them that warmed and comforted him almost more than the cheery blaze of the fire.

"Where's your good man?" he asked her, wanting to hear her voice again. "Is he working out in the fields?"

"No, sir: he died two year agon. He was a thatcher." She indicated the roof of the cottage. "He was a master craftsman. His work has kept me and the children warm and dry."

"Ah, you have children? Where are they now?"

"Grown up and left home. Except for…"

Her voice died away and Carlyon saw a curtain of sadness come down over her eyes and then spread to her mouth, pulling in her lips. He nodded in sympathy, understanding how she could be sad if she was on her own. In his own way, he knew such sadness.

When he had finished eating, May took away his bowl to clean it. While she was doing that, he sat to consider. It was pleasant to sit there. He was being shown such kindness, and at a time when he needed it. Hospitality in a lord's castle would have been more extensive, but it would not have been more sincere, nor more readily given. He wondered how there could be such great differences in rank. Was it only wealth? Were people really all the same, if fine clothes and possessions were stripped away? He looked around him. There was little in the cottage, and yet it seemed so comfortable. Should he stay? Lethargy held him there. It was as if his limbs were encased in leaden greaves, even though he knew that he had to leave and make haste to the Wirral. There was a fuzziness in his head, and he had to keep his cloak around him to keep himself from shivering, in spite of the pleasant glow of the fire. As he sat and stared into the flames, they seemed to carry him away, as if they were a winged boat. His thoughts swayed and revolved through his mind and then gradually he was in the middle of his previous night's dream. The events came back to him once more and he remembered how real it had all seemed. Perhaps it had been real. Perhaps he had seen spirits, or even real people. He could remember touching them as firmly as he was touching his knees now.

A clatter from the other side of the cottage, where May was preparing some household matter, pulled his head round. Dreams and thoughts jumbled together, and he sighed. Making an effort, he reached down and picked up his bag, intending to check what he had with him and whether it would suffice for the rest of his journey. One of the first things he pulled out was Mary's little casket. He had forgotten that he had packed that, but his heart pattered to know that he still had something of hers to remember her by. Letting his bag slip back to the floor, he held the casket on his lap with both hands cradling it, and melancholy thoughts of Mary began to wreathe through his head. He made no attempt to stop them, painful though they were. He opened the casket and looked inside. It was empty, except for a scarf. He took it out and began to run it gently through his fingers. Somehow it seemed to bring Mary back to him, even though he knew that she was lost to him.

At first, immersed in his abstraction, he didn't hear May's cry of surprise. When she called again, he looked up and saw that she was standing beside him. Excitedly, she indicated the scarf, her whole body pressing forward.

"That's my daughter's scarf. Look!" She reached out and held up a corner. "I did that embroidery for her. She'll be in terrible danger if she's lost it. How did you come by it, sir?"

"Are you Mary's mother?" Carlyon asked, surprise jolting him to his feet. "I can scarce believe this. She was such a help to me. I found her in a cottage. She was being held prisoner by a man called Thomas."

"I knew it was something of that kind. When she went missing, her brothers and sister went looking for her, but couldn't find her. Where is this cottage? We must rescue her."

"No, mistress, I had already done that. I took her with me to bring her back to her brother's house, but I was being pursued by an evil witch. I was foolish and the witch took Mary away. It was all my fault. I caught the witch and tried to make her say where Mary was, but she refused, so I killed her. Now Mary is lost and I'm to blame. I know not where she is or even if she still lives."

"Alive she must be. I would know, if she were dead. But we can find her. The scarf will help us." She took the scarf from Carlyon's unresisting fingers and unfurled it by holding two corners. Seemingly satisfied with what she saw, she went across to the table. There she picked up a pail and tipped some water into a bowl. Carlyon watched as she laid the scarf in the bowl, smoothing it out as it soaked up the water. Then she stared at it intently, seeming to sway as she did so. At last she said, "Mary is alive, but she's imprisoned in a stone coffin in an underground cavern. She's no more than a day's journey away from here."

In his joy at hearing that, Carlyon opened his mouth as if about to shout, but May was still speaking. He listened carefully as she described where Mary was to be found and how to get there.

Excitement made his body tremble, overcoming the chill that he was feeling. He was sure that May was right and that her daughter was still alive. He would be able to save her.

"I'll go and bring her back to you," he said, his voice hoarse with emotion.

May looked at him doubtfully and he pulled himself up, setting his face grimly.

"It was my fault that imprisoned her and there's no one else to release her," he insisted. "I know where to go. I will succeed."

May nodded and smiled in her acceptance. She told him that she would prepare him some food for his journey, so that he could leave immediately. While she was doing that, he checked his sword and, with some reluctance, pulled on his boots. They were still damp, but had warmed up a lot and his feet soon felt comfortable in them. When he was ready to leave, May gave him some final instructions, together with Mary's scarf, which she had wrung out and folded neatly. She told him to carry the scarf inside his tunic and to touch it if he should feel doubtful or troubled. He put it away, and then looked at her standing hopefully before him.

"I'll bring Mary back to you, I swear it," he told her.

She nodded her head and held out her hands. He took hold of them, but when he did so, an anxious look crossed her face. She disengaged one of her hands and reached up to place it on his brow. He felt the pleasant coolness on the hot skin and wanted to stay like that, even though he also wanted to be on his way. May's touch was so comforting that he almost forgot the task ahead of him. He felt a pang of disappointment when she took her hand away.

"You have a fever, sir," she said. "One moment." She went briskly to her cupboard and took out a small pot. Carefully she tipped something out of it into a cup of water and gave it to him. "Drink this," she ordered. "It'll help you."

As if his will was not his own, he did as he was told and swallowed the bitter-tasting potion. It seemed to make no difference to how he was feeling, but May told him that he would soon feel better. Slightly reassured, he picked up his bag and set off. As he strode down the road, taking in the fresh air, his head became clearer. Almost immediately, he started to look forward to his mission. Eagerness quickened his step and, although it subsequently slowed to a more reasonable pace, he made good time.

It was wanting a half-hour to sunset and already darkening when he reached the place he sought. He realised with a wry acceptance that he had passed not too far by it only the other day; unknowing how close he had been to Mary. Casting about, driven by a boiling urgency in his blood, he found an ancient oak tree. Age had hollowed out its interior and, walking round it, he found a narrow fissure in its trunk. It was large enough to insert his fist and arm, but no more; yet he knew that that was the way in. May had told him that the witch had taken Mary in there and then closed up the tree.

Carlyon swallowed the saliva in his mouth and then determinedly licked his lips. As if to test, he pulled at the gnarled and solid bark of the fissure. It was immovable. He stood back and looked. It came to him that if he climbed the tree, he would perhaps be able to get down inside the hollow. Wasting no more time, he used irregularities in the fissure to reach the first bough, which was just above his head. From there it was easier and he was soon in the crown. As he had hoped, he could see down into the heart of the tree. Angry despair gripped him when he realised that the opening was still just too narrow for him to squeeze his body through. Then he bethought himself of his sword. Awkwardly amongst the branches, he unsheathed it. His stance was precarious, but he managed to give himself room to swing. He sliced at the opening, intending to cut off pieces. However, on the first hit enough was taken off to admit him easily. Conquering the surprise that almost made him fall, he tied to a stout branch the rope he had brought, and climbed down.

He was carried well into the roots, and by the time his feet touched solid earth, he was in darkness, apart from a bare glimmer of light, which now seemed far above him. Lighting the small oil lamp which May had provided, he straightened up. Carefully he looked around the cramped chamber in which he found himself, sniffing at the dank, earthy smell. There was no sign of Mary, but he saw a narrow passage leading slightly downwards. Squeezing himself through the opening, he went down it. The passage got no larger. Almost immediately the soil gave way to limestone, and in places the passage was so low or narrow that he wondered if he was going the correct way. It seemed to be growing warmer and he began to perspire, although it was impossible to tell whether it was from the closeness of the atmosphere or concern for Mary. Sweat hung on his brow like ropes of falling dew, but he ignored it. Then, after little more than a quarter of an hour of feeling his way cautiously along, the passage opened out into a series of comfortably large caverns. These he recognised from May's description, and he confidently strode through, holding his lamp high.

At last he found what he was seeking. On a low ledge at the side of a cavern, almost as if it had been made for it, there lay a stone in the shape of a coffin. When Carlyon looked more intently, he saw that it was indeed a coffin. It had been rudely planed and constructed out of wood and was now becoming calcified. He looked round it, even pulled it slightly outwards, but there appeared to be no way of opening it. It seemed as solid as rock; as hard as evil.

He stood back and pulled out his sword again. This time he had ample room to swing. He raised it above his head, and then he paused. A weaselly doubt about the strength of the steel on the stone crept into his mind. He moved his head, as if to shake it away, and briefly put his hand to his chest to touch Mary's scarf. His sword was all that he had. That and his faith. Taking a breath and gathering his strength, he brought the blade down on the coffin with full force. There was a loud bang. When he looked, he saw a small crack running across the top of the coffin. He raised the sword and brought it down again. This time there was a clear gap. Bringing close the lamp, he peered in. It was difficult, but by moving his light about, he managed to see inside. He was sure that he could see a human body lying there. Renewed zeal straightened his back and strengthened his arms. He lifted the sword as high as he could. With all his strength, he brought it down again for the third time. The steel clanged on the stone and the lid was cleft asunder.

Carefully he lifted away the two pieces, and when he held his light to look inside the coffin, he saw Mary lying there. Her lids were closed over her soft, beautiful blue eyes. He feared at first that he had arrived too late. Then he noticed that her breast was rising and falling gently, and relief almost made him sink to his knees. For a few seconds he looked at her loveliness as she lay sleeping under the witch's spell. Her slightly parted lips seemed to be speaking to him, inviting him, and a desire to kiss her brought a swirl into his stomach. He stayed his urge, though. Without even formulating the thought, he would not take advantage of her. Nor would he be unfaithful to Patrina. Even so, when he bent his head over the coffin, as if to get close to her, his shadow moved and lightly kissed Mary's mouth. She remained oblivious, locked in her trance.

Carlyon quickly drew back. He knew what he had to do. Urgently he put his hand into his bag and pulled out a small bottle which May had given to him. Taking out the stopper, he reached into the coffin to slide his free arm beneath Mary's neck. Carefully he lifted her unmoving head and, cradling her thus, put the bottle to her lips. A little of the liquid went into her mouth, then a little more. He gently lowered her head and removed his arm. For a few seconds he watched, but there was no change, and he turned and sat on the floor with his back against the cavern wall. May had told him that her remedy would take time to counteract the witch's potion, so he wrapped his cloak round him and settled down to wait. Insensibly, his head began to hang lower, and before he knew it, his exhaustion had sent him to sleep.

# 17

 $\mathcal{T}$ ime passed uncounted, and when Carlyon awoke he was in darkness, the oil in his lamp having burned out. He jerked his head up and immediately remembered where he was. Silence enfolded him like a heavy cloak. Straining, he heard nothing in the black air. It was as if he were alone. Quickly he felt in his bag for his flint and a rushlight and struck a spark. Anxiously he clambered to his feet to look in the coffin. Mary was still lying there, but he saw that she had changed position and was breathing more regularly than before. Colour had come back into her face. It was as if she were now asleep, instead of drugged.

"Mary!" he cried. "Mary! Can you awaken?"

She stirred and he called again, a little more loudly and insistently. This time her eyes opened. She seemed to recognise him straight away, as if she had expected to see him, and a warm smile suffused her face with a radiant beauty, grateful and loving. She lifted her arms to him, and with his free arm he helped her to sit up.

"Oh, I thank the Lord you're safe!" he said. "I've been so worried. I thought it was all my fault."

"I'm safe now. It was a great evil power that was ranged against us, but it's been overcome."

Her voice was a little hoarse, but Carlyon was overjoyed to hear it. He placed the rushlight on the broken coffin lid and then used both hands to help her to climb out. He babbled still in his joy, but when she was on her feet, she gently asked him for some water. Apologetic for his thoughtlessness, he quickly gave her some and waited in silence until she lowered the flask and sweetly smiled her thanks.

"How did you find me?" she asked curiously.

"Your mother told me where you were. Yes! I've been with your mother." He told her how he had found his way to her mother's cottage, although he said nothing of his visions of that night. Then, delightedly, he explained how her mother had discovered where she was. Finally, he paused and told her with an unhappy tone what had happened to James.

Mary rested against the edge of the coffin and sorrow filled her sweet eyes as she looked at Carlyon. "If it was to come to pass, then so it must be," she said. "He was a brave boy. We were truly stalked by the evil one, but at least she's no more."

"Indeed. But do you know how you came to be here? What is this place?"

"I know of such as these. They used to be the habitations of sprites and other wicked imps. They would come out at night to poison cattle, to disarrange household effects, even to spread evil amongst men and women. Perhaps there still are such, but I doubt that you and I need to fear them. We can find our way out now."

She shivered slightly and flexed her muscles to roll away any remaining stiffness. Carlyon picked up the rushlight and held it high while he looked around. He was nervously checking whether they were alone, but he was determined to brave any danger to save Mary. There was nothing there, however, and he offered Mary an arm to hold. Confidently, he led her through the caverns to the passageway which would lead them to the surface. There they had to go in single file. Carlyon held the light and Mary held his belt. He kept up an encouraging conversation, but this was brought to an abrupt end when their passage opened out into a cavern. That should not have happened, and confusion stayed Carlyon's steps.

He turned to Mary, who was looking at him in surprise. "I think we may have been led astray. Perhaps by the evil imps."

"There may be several passages here. You'll have taken the wrong one, I'll warrant."

"We must go back." He looked doubtfully at the narrow passage from which they had just emerged. It seemed a long way to return, and a cold fear made him pause, even though it was unformed.

Mary seemed equally doubtful. "We may not be able to find our way back. If there's magic here, then things may have changed since you came in. Better may be to go forward."

"But which way?" He held the torch as high as he could and looked at the shadows, which might have been irregularities in the limestone or entrances to passages.

"Look, a mouse!" whispered Mary, touching his arm to attract his attention.

He looked and saw the grey rodent scampering into a shadowed part of the wall.

"We'll let that creature choose for us," Mary went on. "I'm sure it knows the way."

Carlyon wasted no time, having no intention of ignoring Mary's advice. Moving to the wall, he saw that there was indeed a passageway. The roof was low. He almost had to stoop, but after allowing Mary to grasp his belt once more, he entered the passage. He led the way along; the width and height of the passage changing, but at no point becoming impassable. After a while he began to doubt that they were going the right way. It did not seem like the way that he had taken when he had come to the caverns. Mary spoke encouraging words, but his limbs were beginning to ache and his body was feeling uncomfortably hot. He was just thinking that they would never find their way back to the upper world, when he glimpsed the mouse once more. It scurried off into the darkness and he wondered if it was leading them to safety or simply running away from them in fear.

Mary told him to trust, and they carried on. After a short while the floor became more heavily littered with stones, so that they had to pick their way carefully. Carlyon now had another worry. The rushlight was nearing its end. He knew that he had one more in his belt; yet the thought of being in darkness in that place was a clammy cloth on his heart. Then, all of a sudden, he noticed that his light was flickering. At first he feared that it was about to die, but then he thankfully realised that it was a draught which was fanning the flame. He mentioned as much to Mary and she cheerfully urged him on.

"We don't have far to go now, I'm sure of it."

They pressed on and found that their way was leading them upwards at last. The breeze also became more noticeable. Before long they found themselves in a narrow cave; almost a cleft. This brought them once more out into the open air. To Carlyon's surprise, dawn was breaking. It was a grey and cold one, but it was a welcome sight. At the edge of the cave, on the slight slope, he looked around him at the nearby countryside. It was still difficult to see, but he recognised nothing. They had come out at a different place from where he had entered the system of caves.

Mary pointed off to the left. "See – a cottage, there. We'll ask for directions and perhaps get some food."

They discovered that they were not far out of their way and, after refreshment, set off to walk back to May's cottage. Their spirits were high and Carlyon refused to acknowledge the ache that was gripping his muscles. He told himself that he would rest fully when he had delivered Mary safely home, and then he would be able to resume his search. His determination kept him putting one foot in front of the other, even after a sleety rain set in. Despite Mary's protestations he took off his cloak and put it over her, refusing to relinquish his responsibilities after having saved her again. For himself, he held his bag on his head to give him some protection, although the icy chill of the sleet still soaked his clothes. He shrugged it off, happy to be with Mary again and eager to set her mother's mind at rest.

Two hundred miles farther south a wedding was being arranged which would unite the Denneton and Cerre-nore families. The earl's retainers had been working steadily at the preparations, driven by their master. Lady Patrina observed all of this activity with a mixture of nervousness and excited anticipation. When her father had first spoken of the marriage, as he lay in his bed after his accident, she had not taken his emphatic tone too seriously. That was his way of speaking, and since she had been a little girl, she had learned that his mind often changed. Things went differently with this matter, however. Her father sent a messenger to Sir John's father and the two men arranged to meet. Sir John went home on the day after Twelfth Night, but until he left, he had been behaving as if they were already betrothed. For her part, Patrina had treated him no differently than she had before, because part of her was still unwilling to believe in the seriousness of the betrothal. It was as if she were in a wagon being pulled by a strong-willed horse over which she had lost control.

She did make an attempt to take back the reins before her father met with Sir John's. He had called her into his chamber to tell her what was being planned. She listened with her head held down and her gaze fixed thoughtfully on the floor at her feet. Then she lifted her head and looked imploringly at her father.

"Must I wed so soon, Papa?"

The earl seemed surprised at the question. "If it's decided, then there seems no reason for delay. Sir John is willing, and it would be well to wed soon if he intends to go abroad with the King this season."

"I feel nervous about taking this step. Are you sure Sir John is a good man?"

"Of course. 'Sblood! He has every good quality a man would desire. Does he frighten you? Well, I can understand a maid being nervous before such a man as Sir John. It's a maid's nature to be timid. But there's no harm."

"I can do what a woman has to do, Papa. When that comes. But I would that the wedding were delayed until Easter."

"Hah! Of course! I see now. You're thinking about Sir Carlyon. He's wandering in the wilderness, and who knows if he'll return?" The earl's face softened. "Dream of him if you will, my dear, but he'll not be a husband for you. I would not force you to marry a man against your will, but you have no objections to Sir John, I ween?"

"No, not in that way. Yet I did promise to make no decision until Sir Carlyon returned."

"As your father, I absolve you of that promise. If Sir Carlyon returns, he'll understand. 'Sblood, Patsy, I've set my heart on Sir John as your husband. All will be well. Come Candlemas, we'll celebrate the wedding."

He pulled her to him and kissed her fondly. Then she was dismissed, but while she walked back to the ladies' quarters, her brow was furrowed as she thought things over. She was not unwilling to marry Sir John, but Sir Carlyon was still tugging at her heartstrings. However, there was no way to contact him. She could only hope that he returned before the end of the month. And what then? Could she choose between the two men? That would be difficult. She often compared them. They were so different, and yet so alike. Sometimes she felt as though they were the two halves of the same person, each supplying what the other lacked. It would be hard for her to choose between them. Perhaps it was as well that her father had chosen for her. She could feel that the matter was out of her hands.

On the evening before the wedding was due to take place, excitement was winding Patrina up, so that she found it difficult to stay still. Two of her closest friends were keeping her company, and in their own pleasure they were doing little to dampen down her excitement.

"Are you happy?" one of them asked her, somewhat pointlessly.

"Oh, I am." Patrina almost hugged herself in her delight. "It's strange to think that this time a year since, I had no thoughts of marriage. Even when my father began to talk about it last Michaelmas, I would that it all be delayed. Yet here we are now on the eve of my wedding and I would that it were already tomorrow eve. I doubt I'll sleep this night."

Her friends giggled, and a tender blush spread over Patrina's face as she realised what they were thinking.

"It'll be a marvellous thing to be the mistress of my own house, to have my own keys and to run my own household. You'll both be able to visit me, and I shall entertain you."

Her friends clapped their hands in excitement and spoke about such visits. From there the conversation wandered to the people who would be attending the wedding celebration. While they were discussing the guests, one of Patrina's friends slyly mentioned that one person would be missing.

"I wonder what Sir Carlyon will be doing tomorrow?" she explained.

The quest was well known amongst Patrina's friends, and now that it had been mentioned, Patrina sighed in a ladylike fashion, as if an insubstantial shadow of sadness had fluttered by. "I also have been thinking of him and wondering where he may be. I dreamed of him but the other night."

"Have you not heard how he is?"

"I've heard nothing since the morn he went away without a farewell to me. It's not known if he's well, or even still alive." Patrina reached out for her shawl of sadness again. It was almost as if she felt that she had to wear such an aura.

Her friends too were thoughtful. One broke the short silence that had fallen by remarking that he had been away for many weeks.

"I thought me that he would be back by New Year's Day with my flowers," said Patrina. "I can't keep waiting. Who can know how long I'll have to wait? No one would expect me to wait forever."

Her friends nodded.

"I told Sir Carlyon I couldn't decide between him and Sir John, and that I'd look favourably on him if he brought me my desire. I was not to know that Sir John would do a brave service for me by saving my father from danger. Now, even if Sir Carlyon had returned, I would not know how to choose between them. So my father has chosen, and there's an end to it. I can do no more, will I or not."

The next morning, when a fire was burning in her small hearth and she was sitting on her stool in a tub of warm water, she wanted to stay there. She wanted to keep things just as they were, even though another part of her was eagerly desiring the day's activities and what they would bring. In uncustomary irritation she scolded her maid, Matty, when she accidentally splashed her while adding another jug of hot water to the bath. Matty, unused to such behaviour, having been with her mistress for many years, drew back in shame and apologised profusely. Patrina saw the hurt in her face and cut her short. She knew that she was blaming her unjustly.

"Forgive me," she said, offering her a smile. "My mind is not my own this day. I don't know what I want or don't want."

"Of course, my lady. It's an exciting time. I too am feeling nervous at what's to come."

"I'm glad you'll be with me when I go to my new home. I want to be with Sir John, but I don't want to be on my own."

Patrina stopped, knowing that she was expressing herself badly. She didn't know how to express the strange feelings running through her like inquisitive mice. Closing her eyes slightly, she lifted the cake of soap to her nose and gently sniffed the calming perfume. Matty took up a damp linen rag and tenderly began to rub her back. For a while Patrina soaked sensuously in a private world.

Afterwards, Matty helped her on with her wedding gown. The warm silk rustled around her and, lovingly, Patrina felt its soft smoothness with her fingers. The dressmaker had fitted the bodice exactly to her slim figure, and when Matty had fastened it up, Patrina took a few steps, swirling her body in half-turns to test the comfort of the gown and to luxuriate in the wide-cut skirt which fell in folds to her feet and then trailed in a train along the floor behind her. Matty waited patiently, and when Patrina caught her eye, she saw that her maid was looking at her approvingly, seemingly as excited as she was. Patrina smiled fondly at her, but then they were interrupted by the entry of Patrina's two friends, who had finished dressing and had come to be with the bride. Some time was spent in admiration and excited chatter, but finally Patrina covered her head with a plain veil which she had borrowed from her aunt, and allowed one of her friends to place a circlet of gold round her temples to hold it in place. At last she was ready, and she stood to allow herself to be complimented. Suddenly she wanted to embrace her friends. She was embarking on a journey that could not be changed, and that realisation chilled her momentarily, as if an icy north wind had blown through the room.

When the time came for the ceremony to begin, her nervousness had returned, but she composed herself. It was exciting, after all, and she knew that it was what she wanted. When her father called her to him, she went out firmly and stood between him and John. With a demure expression, she looked at the assembled guests as her father began his wedding address.

"Dear cousins, dear friends, I've asked you all here on the occasion of the marriage of my beloved daughter, Patrina, to Sir John."

Patrina listened as her father praised her virtues and accomplishments, and she looked over the crowd filling the hall, noticing how all of the faces were smiling and happy. At last her father paused briefly, before saying that both Patrina and John were agreeable to the marriage and that he called upon all those present to witness their promises.

John made his in a loud and authoritative voice which reached out to all parts of the hall, ending confidently with, "And thereto I plight you my troth."

Patrina raised her head, feeling nervous, but ready to speak. Her mouth opened, but before a sound came out, there was a clatter that made her jump. A shutter at the window behind them had banged back against the wall, as if it had been caught by a gust of wind. A white swan's feather blew in. Swooping gently, it fluttered almost as far as Patrina before sinking weakly to the floor. However, no one seemed to notice that in the disturbance caused by the bang. Patrina laughed in surprise, and then made her promise in a clear voice that most of the guests were able to hear.

As if released from a pen, the guests pressed forward, eager with their congratulations and good wishes. Patrina was now a married woman and, standing by John's side, she gracefully received the warm embraces and kisses. Then, hand in hand, Patrina and John led them in a merry procession to the church, where the priest was waiting for them at the door. When everyone had crowded round and settled down, he raised his arms and blessed the couple.

After asking if both parties had consented to the marriage, he turned and all followed him into the church, where he conducted the nuptial Mass.

When they came out to return home, John set a fast pace, his long strides covering the ground quickly. By his side, Patrina was almost trotting as she strove to keep up with him. Her heavily soiled train dragged along the road behind her and seemed to be pulling her back, as if trying to delay her return.

"You're making much haste, my lord," she said breathlessly.

"I want to eat. I fancy dinner will be ready and waiting for us. We've wasted time enough. It's the hour for the feasting and celebration to begin."

This feasting and merriment carried on for the rest of the day. John did not spend a lot of time with Patrina after they left the table, seeming to prefer roistering with his male companions. She was a little unhappy about that, but her female relatives and friends almost made up for it. Before the dancing began, she and John ate some cake together, laughingly feeding each other pieces, and then they exchanged rings. John also gave her a gift of a pure white silk mantle, and her pleasure flowed over her face like sunlight.

"Thank you, my lord, how lovely! How did you guess what would please me?"

"My mother had it made for me. I don't know about such fripperies," he said dismissively.

Patrina had spent some time in deciding on a gift for him, and had at last had made a small knife with its haft inlaid with ivory and diamonds. When she gave it to him, his eyes lit up and he examined it almost fondly. She could tell that she had made a good choice and that he was pleased with it, because he was so enthralled that he neglected to thank her for it. However, as the musicians struck up a carole, he formally asked her for a dance and she happily allowed herself to be led out.

# 18

Carlyon was lying on a straw mattress in a simple one-roomed cottage in the north-west of England. Although he was unaware of it, he was slipping in and out of consciousness. He had been drenched by icy water once too often and the threatening fever had finally laid its clammy grip upon him. After he had rescued Mary from the underground cavern where she had been placed by the witch, they had walked back to her mother's house in good spirits, despite the sleet which set in. It was a happy walk, although an aching weariness began to drag at Carlyon's bones, slowing his pace.

Early in the afternoon, Mary stopped and pulled him to a halt. "This is not good," she said. "You're shivering. It can't go on."

"What?! I'm but cold. I'll rest when I get you home."

"That won't happen if you don't wrap yourself from this weather. See how you tremble. You must share this cloak with me."

He still refused. Obstinacy was preventing him from thinking properly, but Mary was firm. She ignored his protests and finally he allowed her to spread the cloak over the two of them. Underneath it she put an arm round his waist to pull him closer, and her warm body was a comfort to him.

May's joy at their return was immediately tempered with concern when she saw Carlyon's condition. He smiled weakly at her. He wanted to share her pleasure at being reunited with Mary, but was defeated by a desire for rest. He allowed himself to be hurried into the cottage, and he offered no resistance when he felt May begin to undress him. Down to his shift, he stood there shivering, unable to move or to think for himself. She wrapped him in a soft linen sheet and then laid him down on her bed before covering him with a thick woollen blanket. She gave her daughter a cloth with some cold water to bathe his forehead, but by that time he was asleep.

Afterwards he remembered Mary sitting by him, soothing and wiping him, but he was confused as to what was real and what was a dream. He thought he remembered being made to drink a bitter herbal concoction, but again it was jumbled in with fantastic images that surely had no root in reality. He was creeping down dark passages. He was fighting faceless creatures with long teeth and curved claws. He was seeking, seeking, driven by a fear that he would never find what he had lost. Sometimes Patrina was wiping his face with a cool cloth, and even though she looked like Mary, it did not seem odd to him.

Then he was aware of lying on a straw mattress. His eyes were closed, but he could hear something. It seemed unimportant and he did not want to move. Slowly, almost lazily, his eyes opened. He saw that the noise was coming from a fire on which a pot was bubbling gently, and he remembered that he was in May's cottage. As the memory of how he had got there flowed silently back into his mind, he saw that Mary was lying on the floor between him and the fire. He wanted to raise his head to look more closely, but there was no strength in his shoulders and when he tried to call her, only a soft whisper came out of his mouth.

"Ssh, now. Lie calmly." The voice came from out of his range of vision, but before he could gather his strength to move his head, May was at his bedside. She bent over him and put her hand on his forehead. "That's better," she soothed. "You must rest now. I think all your strength has gone."

"Mary," he managed to say at last. "What's she doing?"

"She's well. Worry not. She sleeps, so make no noise. She's had but scant rest since you returned."

He wanted to get up, and to ask more questions, but it was too much effort. It seemed easier just to lie there. May brought him some warm milk and lifted him up to cradle him in her arms while he drank it. She had put in a herbal powder, and he felt better after finishing it. When she laid his head, as gently as a babe's, back on the pillow, he was ready to speak.

"What's been happening?" he asked.

"You've had a fever. For three days and nights. I've never seen one like it. I thought that even my potions would not serve. Mary stayed by your side, calming you and changing your covers. I couldn't persuade her to leave you. Early this morn the fever broke and at last I convinced her you would be well and she could rest."

Carlyon lay back and licked his milky lips while he considered this. He tried to remember, but there were only snatches. There was travelling back with Mary. That he could remember. They had been happy, but then everything was an insubstantial fog and, try as he might, his fingers of memory could not hold it. He recalled nothing of their arrival at the cottage. Even the moments of lucidness during the fever had drifted out of reach. "I remember nought of reaching here."

"I scarce wonder at that. You were delirious with the fever. As fortune willed, I'd sent for my sons and one of them came upon you on the way, not a league distant. Mary was almost carrying you, and I doubt she would have managed had her brother not met the two of you."

Carlyon turned his head to look at the sweetly sleeping Mary, and affection for her almost made him close his eyes. He wished that he knew what had been happening over the past few days. It was as if he was missing something; something that he needed to know about. He looked back at May. "I knew nought of that. I must thank your son. Where is he?"

"Both of my sons have had to leave, but Mary's sister is still here until the morrow. They are all beholden to you for what you've done for Mary. She's told us everything. We shall be forever grateful to you."

"Mary has repaid any debt a hundredfold. I owe her my life also."

As he said that, tiredness began pressing on his eyelids and May pulled up his blanket. She told him to rest, and he drifted back into sleep.

When he awoke later that afternoon, his mind was clear. He knew where he was and he could remember how he had got there. The period of his fever was beyond recall, but May's explanation of it was still there. Weakness swaddled his body like a tight sheet, but he managed to turn his head to look at where Mary had been lying near the fire. The mattress had been taken up and she was no longer there. He wondered momentarily if his memory was imperfect, but as his eyes moved, he saw her. She was sitting at the table underneath a window, and by its light she was darning a gown. For a few seconds he studied her and his brow furrowed in puzzlement. She seemed older, as if years had passed since he'd last seen her; as if he had been insensible for a long time. Fearful that magic was holding him, he tried to move, but his physical lassitude only allowed a little restlessness. This seemed to attract his companion's attention. She looked over at him and smiled – the same beautiful smile that he remembered. Before he could speak, she turned her head away and called.

"Mama! Mary! He's awake now!"

Carlyon looked in the same direction and saw May come into the cottage, closely followed by Mary. Glancing back at the other woman, still sitting at the table, he realised that she must be Mary's elder sister, and relief relaxed his body. Mother and younger daughter fussed by his bed, and their happiness caressed him. He smiled contentedly in response and, in reply to their expressions of concern, said that he was feeling much better. He did feel comfortable, but when he tried to raise himself, thinking to sit up, the effort was too much and as he sank back, a sharp breath was forced from his lungs.

"There now," said May. "Don't try yet. Still more time."

"You've lost so much strength," Mary added. "But you'll get it back." She looked at her mother. "Shall I try him with some broth now?"

"No harm, I trow. He may take."

Carlyon listened to them talking about him, but he barely took it in. He was looking at Mary, as if her simple presence was feeding strength to him. She was, as always, wearing a plain woollen gown, but her mother had put her long brown hair into braids for her. These framed her face neatly. He watched her move quickly to the fire and ladle some liquid into a bowl from a pot that was hanging there. When she came back, May sat at the head of the bed and held him up, so that her daughter could put the bowl to his lips. He had no appetite, but to please Mary he took some into his mouth. It seemed to have no savour, but he swallowed it down and she continued putting the bowl to his lips. The bowl was almost empty when May said that he'd had enough and told Mary to give him some water. Then she lowered his head back onto the pillow and he let Mary wipe his mouth with a damp cloth.

"Thank you," he said softly. "I'll rest again now."

For what remained of the day, he watched the three women go about their household tasks, occasionally replying to a comment, but satisfied just to let things revolve around him. When everyone settled down for the night, he slept restlessly. Now that he was no longer held by his fever, he was fully sensible of the aching and stiffness in his joints. He was glad when dawn came and he was put up into a sitting position. This time he was able to hold himself against a pillow which Mary placed between him and the wall, and he spent a comfortable day. By evening he was lifting himself up in the bed or lying down again as he willed. His appetite was still elusive, but he enjoyed being fed by Mary or even being given a herbal potion prepared by her mother.

Over the following days his strength gradually returned. One afternoon some sunshine attracted him and he went outside the cottage for the first time since his return from Mary's rescue. It was a gentle day, hollowed out of winter. There was still snow lying about, so he did not go far. Holding on to Mary's arm, he found a spot where the sun could warm and revive him. He drew in the crisp air and smiled at his companion.

"How pleasant to be outside again," he said. "I can almost feel that spring is about to break."

"I fear it may be some more weeks yet. But, God willing, you'll be recovered before then. Mama is pleased with how you're doing."

"Her mixtures are doing me good. But your care is the greater medicine. I'll be forever in your debt."

"I in yours also. It may be that some debts can never be repaid."

"Mayhap so. We must be grateful for the mercies that we have."

He reached round with his left hand to touch the fingers of her hand which was holding his right arm to give him support. Gently he squeezed them and felt a pleasant warmth in them. She smiled at him, as if in agreement with what he had said, and he kept his hand where it was as they walked back to the cottage.

Days passed and his recovery continued. He began to help with collecting firewood, and then on some days he was able to go out with a net and snares to catch wildfowl and hares. It was a strangely enjoyable life and he seemed to have no wish to end it. It was as if something magical were keeping him at the cottage. His relations with Mary and her mother were as easy as though he were a member of the family. He never considered questions of rank. Mary used his first name, and she was so comfortable with him that she thought nothing of teasing him if the occasion arose.

One day he had been out with her, helping her to plough their strip in the field, ready for the spring planting, and when they went to the village to return the ox and plough which they had borrowed, the man idly remarked that the two of them made a handsome couple. Mary blushed, and Carlyon, although surprised at the comment, was not offended, but rather pleased. When they walked back to the cottage, which was a little over a mile distant, he could think of nothing to say at first. Mary was the one who began to speak of the next day's work, and they were soon laughing and joking as usual.

They were almost back at the cottage when Mary, looking at him as she said something, failed to notice a muddy patch on the slope down which they were walking. Her foot slipped, and she would have fallen, had he not caught her. They both laughed at the incident, but he kept his arms round her, happy at the soft tenderness of her body against the stocky strength of his. Suddenly they fell silent and looked at each other in the twilight. A pigeon in a nearby tree was cooing as it settled down for the night, but Carlyon barely noticed. He was looking at Mary's face, slightly below his and partly in shadow. Almost without thought he bent his head and pressed his mouth against hers. As their lips touched, he felt a wonderful surge, as if they were both being lifted off their feet. He had never before experienced such a marvellous sensation. When he drew his head back, he looked at her and smiled. She lowered her eyes demurely, but made no other movement. Then abruptly, unwanted, a feeling that he was being unfaithful to Patrina seemed to grip his shoulders. It was as if her spirit had spoken to him. He loosened his grip and released Mary. Taking a step away from her, he looked in the direction of the cottage.

"We should be getting on. It's almost dark," he said gruffly.

Mary seemed to sense that he had gone away from her, and she nodded sadly. "Verily so. We must get back," she agreed, and he glanced at her sharply, surprised at the practicality which she had forced into her tone. She went on. "Mama will have supper ready. I'll warrant you're as hungry as I am."

For the few remaining minutes of their walk, Mary spoke as if nothing had happened. This calmed Carlyon and he spent a comfortable evening. He also had a comfortable night. Lying in the darkness after they had all retired, he could hear Mary and her mother in the bed on the other side of the curtain. He tried to think about Mary and his feelings for her, but his day's work had built up in him an insidious tiredness. Sleep quickly stopped up his eyes and he knew nothing until he was woken at dawn.

Over breakfast, he told the women that he would go out hunting that day and see if he could get some partridge. It was just an excuse so that he could think in solitude, and he saw Mary look at him as if she guessed. However, she said nothing. May also kept to herself whatever thoughts she might have, except for a mention that the wind had changed and so there would be rain later in the day. He smiled ruefully for her benefit and said that he hoped to be back before then.

When he was ready, he strode off down the path, carrying his confidence as if it were a shoulder pack. This had slipped down somewhat by the time that he was out in the woodland. He was trying to concentrate on preparing his snare, but his thoughts kept jumping back to his situation and his intentions. His heart was speaking a language that his head did not understand. It was perfectly clear to him what he should do. He knew his duty. As a gentleman, as a knight, he could not be unfaithful to Patrina, to whom he had made a vow. He sighed to remember how he had made that vow almost without thought, because the proposed search had seemed so symbolic, so romantic. Now he was finding it difficult to see any point to it. However, Patrina would be waiting for him to return. He imagined her in her chamber, perhaps embroidering, perhaps reading. It was almost as if she were in a different world;

a world that had started to become dreamlike to him. She would be dreaming of him and trusting him to be true to her. But he had betrayed her. He had kissed another woman.

Despite himself, he could not prevent himself from feeling pleasure at that kiss. He could still remember clearly how it had melted on his lips like honey. It had seemed to come so naturally, and it had been so enjoyable. He had been kissed by women before, but they had been friendly kisses of greeting. When he had kissed Mary, she had seemed to mould to him, and he remembered with embarrassment how his body had trembled slightly. He hoped that she had not felt it, because he was not one of those men who would take advantage of an inferior. It was so unfortunate that she was only a thatcher's daughter. He could not deny that as a woman she was the equal of Lady Patrina. Perhaps her qualities were even greater. He smiled to himself as he remembered Patrina's flighty and romantic behaviour. It had amused him and he had thought it sweet and childlike. But over the past weeks he had been given an insight into real life, and although he struggled, he was being driven to admit that Patrina's life and behaviour were shallow. He wondered if she would ever grow out of that; if maturity would ever clothe her body. Almost without wishing to, he remembered how she had teased him with John's rivalry. Was that love? Was she even now teasing John with him? Or was she dallying even more deeply? It was with a strange mixture of pleasure and reluctance that he accepted that Mary would be capable of a truer and deeper love than Patrina. Nevertheless, he could not marry Mary. His father would not allow it. Nobody would. Such things just did not happen. The court would be scandalised and would jeer at him. And yet his own family had been low-born not so many generations back. These distinctions of rank were artificial; made by men, not by God. He could live with Mary somewhere away from the court, the two of them in love and contented. His father would be sure to accept Mary eventually. So why should he not marry Mary? He asked himself the question and he answered it for himself. He could not marry Mary because he had pledged his love to Patrina.

While he was wrapped in his ruminations, a honking sound took his ears, as if they were being tugged. He looked up and saw a pair of swans flying over, heading southwards. He stood and watched their effortless flight until he could see them no more. They had reminded him of his duty; of the reason why he was in that part of the country. For some seconds he stood, looking up through the trees. It came to him that if he stayed at May's cottage, he did not know what would happen. It would become more difficult to make a decision.

When they were having supper that evening, he waited and watched for an opportunity to speak. He was determined to do so, but wanted it to seem natural. In the end the words seemed starker than he meant them to, and he tried to soften them with a smile. "I must leave on the morrow. I have a search to complete, you know. I want to find some of the flowers of the swan."

After glancing at Mary, he looked at her mother as he spoke, and it was she who responded first. He saw surprise on her face, and he wondered if she had been reading more into his relationship with her daughter than there was.

"Why do you want to carry on with this...search?" she asked, kindly but firmly. "If you do it, what'll you do then? There's nothing more you can do with it. Will you return south again? There's nought for you there."

He had watched her face while she had been saying that. He knew that there was something for him if he returned south. So he had to complete what he had set out to do.

His attention was distracted by Mary, who rattled her spoon as she put it in her bowl. He had barely looked at her; both fear and shame keeping his head turned away. Now he looked directly into eyes that were limpid with understanding. It was as if she knew that she could not keep him. He wanted to reach across the table to take her hand, but he was being driven by a power that was greater even than her love. Held by her gaze, he was almost surprised when she spoke.

"Must you leave immediately on the morrow? Can you not stay a few days more at least?" Her voice was as gentle as if she were breathing in his ear, and it was not strong enough to change his course.

"No. No. It's best that I complete my task as soon as possible. I made a vow to collect these flowers. I'm yet a knight, and as a knight, I can't break my vow. I must continue. Time is passing."

It was as if he felt a need for urgency, but he did not know why. He smiled a little helplessly at the two women and, in a nervous gesture, lightly squeezed his nostrils between his thumb and forefinger. May looked at him impassively for a couple of seconds. Then she slid off the bench which she was sharing with her daughter, and stood up. She clapped her hands together lightly and rubbed her fingers on the other palm. Looking calmly at Carlyon, she told him that she would give him some directions before he left, and he thanked her, relieved that she seemed to have accepted his decision.

Carlyon's night was restless. It was almost as if he were being continually aggravated by lice. He was glad to be able to get up at dawn and have breakfast with Mary and her mother. He felt that Mary had accepted the fact of his departure and that he had to complete his search. He was alert to any nuances in her behaviour or the tone of her voice, but he picked up no definite change towards him. His behaviour towards her was consciously kind and gentle, but with a slight, undeliberate gauze of patronage. Now that his decision had been made, he was once again a knight.

It was May who seemed to be allowing the situation to weigh on her. She spoke to Mary and Carlyon as she always did, but Carlyon thought that he detected a guardedness in her tone and a thoughtfulness in her movements. Then while they were eating their porridge, she bluntly brought up the topic that was on their minds.

"Do you still mean to leave for the Wirral Forest today?"

"Yes, it must be done. I'll prepare straight after we've eaten."

A slight breath of relief passed through him now that the matter was out in the open. He began to talk about his time with them almost apologetically, but before he had said more than a few words, May interrupted him. He let her discourtesy pass and listened politely.

"You don't have to leave, mind. You can bide here with us till summer. It'll be pleasanter, easier to travel then. There'll be leaves on the trees, plenty of life around. You can look for your flowers then."

It was as if she was giving him another chance to change his mind, but he did not even consider her suggestion. He had a feeling that if he stayed any longer, then perhaps he would never leave. There was a sense of magic in that cottage.

"No," he said. "I must leave now."

May seemed to shrug, but she accepted his decision. She resumed eating her porridge, while Mary remarked that the day looked to be a fine one for travelling. Her mother listened for a minute or two to the conversation that followed, and then said that if Carlyon was wanting to go to the Wirral Forest, he would find it less than two days' journey away. He listened carefully as she gave him some directions, and he thanked her gravely for them. At last he rose from the table and went to complete his preparations for departure. There was sadness at the thought of leaving the happiness of the little cottage and the simple life there, but an eagerness to resume his task was clawing at his heels like an importunate cat. He wanted to be on his way and return to the life which was proper to his station.

May prepared some bread and cheese for his journey. He took the cloth-wrapped package with gratitude; then, before he tied up his bag, Mary came to stand silently before him. He looked up and saw that she was holding a small flask.

"Take this," she told him. "It's water from a spring nearby. I collected it myself and I've said a prayer over it. If you sprinkle some over the flowers of the swan before you take them, it'll keep you safe from any harm."

"Thank you, Mary. Thank you for everything."

"We must thank you, sir," broke in May, before her daughter could answer.

Carlyon looked at her, wondering if she was deliberately interposing herself between him and Mary, but she was smiling fondly at him. It was the same kind of smile that his mother gave him, and he took hold of her hands to say his farewell to her.

"Travel safely," she told him, when he let her hands go, "and I pray you find what you're looking for." She smiled again, and it was almost as though she were blessing him.

He turned to Mary.

"Fare you well, Carlyon," she told him. "May God keep you safe."

Pleased that she still familiarly used his name, he leaned forward to embrace her. She kissed his cheek and he felt her arms squeeze round him. He also pressed her to him with his arms. He had made a decision, but now he was regretting having made it. It was almost as if he wanted to stay standing as he was: he in Mary's arms and she in his. It would be pleasant not to have to do or be responsible for anything. Momentarily he knew that he could abandon his search and stay with Mary, forgetting his old world and forgotten by it, but in that very moment the thought melted like a drop of butter on the tongue. He also knew that he would not do it.

"I would that I could stay," he whispered in her ear, "but I'm being called. I must answer. Fare you well, Mary. I'll never forget this place. I'll never forget you or your mother."

Then he released his hold. He had to leave. He had to find the flowers of the swan and win the lady Patrina. After this, he had a wistful feeling that he would never see Mary again.

# 19

hen Carlyon left May's cottage, he walked along the path through the trees towards the high road with a steady if reluctant step. A whispering air of resignation accompanied him and he could sense the gaze of the two women upon his back. He stopped and turned for a final farewell wave, but it was already too late. The cottage was hidden by the trees. He had delayed too long and he looked in some puzzlement, surprised at how far he had unthinkingly walked. He could not believe it possible. It was almost as if the cottage had disappeared, or as if it had never existed. He shook his head and knew that he could not have imagined it.

Taking a breath, he continued his journey, eager to get it out of the way. When he reached the River Mersey, he found someone to row him across, and on the other side he found himself some lodgings for the night. It was amusing at first to be amongst ordinary people, but he knew that he could not talk to them about all that had befallen him. Even so, he delighted in imagining how he would keep Patrina enthralled when he told her all his tales of adventure. John would be so jealous. Patrina would scarcely believe that so much had happened to him in so short a time.

The following day he set off early. By late forenoon he was well into the forest, and he sat on a fallen tree with his cloak wrapped about him, to eat a little food. Afterwards he looked around, wondering where to walk next. Through the trees he thought that he could see a clearing. He was just thinking of going that way, for want of any better notion, when he heard the beat of wings. A swan was flying over, barely above the treetops. Its flight seemed faltering, and his heart surged with the realisation that this might be the sign for which he was waiting.

He hurried after the swan and saw that it had settled down in a clearing by a small pool. Quietly he hid behind a tree and peeped out. The swan was motionless, huddled in a heap, its whiteness like a ball of snow on the grass. As Carlyon watched, the swan began to move. It drew itself up onto its legs and, stretching out its neck, began to sing. The melody was unlike anything that he had heard before, and yet there was a familiarity to it that soothed his soul and quietened his breath. It began tremulously, and so softly that it was several notes in before his ear picked it up. There was a liquid, rippling note that quickly swelled into a variety of deep and full notes. These were harmonised with low trills and warbles and occasionally a clear, rich whistle, as if from a flute. Carlyon stood there motionless. He could not understand how such complex melodies could come from one throat; nor how the song seemed to be surrounding him, enfolding him. Enthralled, he surrendered himself to its beauty, but it was over all too soon. The swan lowered its neck and sank back down onto the ground. From his hiding place Carlyon watched for several seconds longer, but he knew that the swan had died.

Looking around the clearing, he noticed for the first time strewn patches of white flowers where other swans had died. This was what he had been seeking. This was what he had to take back to Lady Patrina. He walked out into the clearing and over to a clump of the flowers. Still overcome by what he had seen and the magic of what he had heard, he took out his knife and bent to dig up six of the flowers with their roots. He was gathering up moss and grass to wrap them when he suddenly realised that he had been too hasty to remember to sprinkle them with water from Mary's flask. For a moment he paused and looked about him. He was alone, apart from the recently dead swan some yards away from him. The sky was cloudy, but there was plenty of light and he could see without obstruction all around the clearing. A breeze had risen unnoticed and was tossing the cupped heads of the flowers, so that they seemed to be nodding knowingly. There were no animal sounds, no birdsong, just a slight whooshing and rustling of wind. It seemed a little exposed, as if there might be something behind him; something waiting. He looked back at the flowers in his hand and at the sticky soil round their roots, which was staining his fingers. It had been done now.

Hastily, he finished wrapping the flowers. Then he put them into a small leather pouch, careful not to endanger the graceful stems. Equally carefully he placed the pouch in the top of his pack and stood up, lifting the pack and his shield onto his shoulder as he did so. He gave a final glance around the clearing. He was feeling no different from when he had entered it. Perhaps there would be no ill fortune from his memory lapse. He told himself that he would have to make the best of it, whatever befell him. And then, unbidden, the thought was thrust into his mind that the water might not have worked anyway. He looked behind him, as if it had been a devil whispering those ignoble words into his ear, and shook his head angrily. It was wrong of him to countenance such an idea.

Wasting no more time, he crossed himself and set off through the trees, retracing his steps until he found the narrow trackway that had brought him into the forest. He spent the night in the same inn as before, but when he woke up in the morning he decided that instead of taking the road to Chester, he would go back across the River Mersey and call in on Mary and her mother. He thought that they might like to know that he had been successful in his search and had found the flowers. Pleased with this idea, he had a quick breakfast and left as soon as he could.

Across the river he struck out confidently northwards, and by early afternoon he was in an area that he recognised. And yet there seemed to have been changes. He followed paths which he thought he knew, but he could find no trace of May's cottage. He asked people whom he met, but no one had heard of May the thatcher's widow; nor of her daughter. It suddenly came to him that he was not being allowed to find the cottage because he had chosen Patrina before Mary. He stood in thought and then almost smiled at the idea. He pursed his mouth and told himself that he had simply gone astray. It was difficult to pick out landmarks when hills and woods all looked so similar. Struck by a sudden idea, he unfastened the shield from his bag and held it out in front of him.

"Can you help me, Shield? Where is Mary and her mother's cottage?"

He spoke confidently, but the boss did not transform into a face. Dismay tightened his chest as the shield remained inert, without response. He thought to ask again, but stopped. The shield had been of great help to him during his journey, and perhaps it would be again, if he really needed it. He nodded in acceptance. This time he knew that he must rely on his own abilities. Well, he was stronger now and perhaps did not need the shield's help. Even so, he tied it back in place gently, as if it were alive, but his faint hope died as the shield still stayed silent. Disappointed that he would not be seeing Mary again, he nevertheless accepted it and set off in an easterly direction. He would find somewhere to lodge that night, and then on the morrow he would seek out a man who would sell him a horse.

He was still walking when twilight overtook him. Behind him, to the west, the indifferent hills were dyed with fair evening's rose, but before him there was a thickening gloom that seemed to be creeping inexorably towards him. However, he had spotted a cottage, and he strode towards that. As he drew near, he saw that there was a horse hobbled outside, waiting patiently. When he was close enough to think that it was not an ordinary farm horse, the animal lifted its head in his direction and gave a welcoming whinny.

Carlyon gave a start and ran the last few yards. It was Champion. He dropped his bag and put out a hand to touch the horse's flank, as if to convince himself that he was real. Then he put his other hand on the side of the face that was nuzzling at his.

"How came you here, boy? How came you here?"

Champion whinnied his pleasure at seeing his master, and stamped his feet as if eager to leave. Carlyon, also pleased and almost disbelieving, ran his hand along the horse's body, uttering calming words as he did so. Then a noise made him turn his head, and he saw that a man had come out of the cottage. In answer to the man's wary question, Carlyon told him that he was a traveller looking for lodgings.

"I'm also looking for a horse," he added. "Where did you get this one?"

"Ah, he came outta t'forest one day. He'd been attacked by a wild beast or some such. He had many wounds and I thought me he was like to die, but I did what I could and he's recovered now. Except, there on his neck there's a strange wound, as if he was cut by a sword. I've not been able to cure that."

"Hmm, yes." In his embarrassment, Carlyon said no more, but he peered closely at his horse. In the weak twilight, he now saw the wound on the left side of Champion's neck, although he was unable to see how serious it was. Champion snickered, and in his remorse Carlyon thought that it sounded like forgiveness. Then he had an idea. As if being guided, he bent down to his bag and took out the flask which Mary had given to him. Carefully he sprinkled some drops of water onto Champion's neck, praying for his recovery as he did so. When he had put the flask back in his bag, he noticed that the man was watching him curiously.

"D'you know this horse, sir?" the man asked.

"Yes. He was mine, but I lost him in a forest to the north of here. I thank God he's safe and I've found him again. Did he have a saddle on?"

"Aye, I've got it in t'ouse."

Carlyon described it, and the man nodded reluctantly. Joyful at the turn of events, Carlyon asked for a night's lodging and, after seeing that Champion was properly settled, went into the cottage to spend the night with the man and his family. The next morning he went out immediately to check on Champion and found that the neck wound had healed. He had thought that that would be the case, but relief at the magical speed of the recovery pumped a new energy into his veins. Eager to be on his way, he did not haggle when agreeing a satisfactory reward for all that the man had done.

It was a marvellous feeling to be in the saddle again after so long, and Carlyon drew in a deep breath while he looked around him. Champion pranced excitedly in the early morning sunshine, as if he too were happy again. When Carlyon rode off down the lane, one hand was always on the rein, but the other occasionally reached out to stroke his horse's neck.

After a while he came out onto open moorland. He was not far along when he noticed a rider to his left approaching down a road that would intersect with his. There was something familiar about the man, and as Carlyon's idle look turned into curiosity, he realised that the man looked like him. Nervously he glanced ahead at where their paths would meet. When he looked back at the other rider, the sun caught the man's surtout. As if spellbound, Carlyon saw his own device of a white swan's quill. Then suddenly it came to him that the familiarity was because the man was wearing his clothes, and in almost the same moment he saw that the man was his squire, James. Almost disbelieving his eyes, Carlyon drew in a breath and jerked at his reins in his surprise. He saw that James had now recognised him, because he was waving and calling. Both men spurred their horses and cut across the intervening moor, aching to lose no time. When they met, they jumped from their saddles and embraced wildly. They had been shouting questions and exclamations at each other as they had ridden up, but after their embrace James gave way to his master and let him breathlessly ask again how he was there safe and sound.

"I thought you had perished in killing the witch."

"I almost did so." James closed his eyes momentarily, as if shaken by the memory, but he went on. "She was difficult to kill. I thought I never would. She wouldn't stay under the water and I had to lie on her. The armour pulled me down also, and I was like to drown with the witch. Mayhap I did. I remember nothing of how I escaped, but I found me lying on the bank. It may be that an angel helped me out of the pond. I know not. I only know I was alive, but I doubt me I was in my right mind. I got up and I wandered across the moor, heedless of where I was going. Good fortune guided me and I came upon a monastery. The brothers took me in, but it seems that I knew nothing, not even my name."

"Is this so?" asked Carlyon, pain at James's tale twisting his face.

"Very true. I was as if bewitched. I was in their infirmary for many days, and when I recovered my strength I did work in the monastery to help the brothers. I prayed with them also, and gradually my memory began to return. I was able to tell the prior why I had been wandering on the moor. I set off two days ago to search for you, and praise be, I've found you. But what of Mary? Are you still seeking her?"

"No – I was able to find her and take her safely back to her mother." Carlyon told James briefly what had happened and how he had left them to go and seek the flowers of the swan. "At last I found them, and I was able to get some to take back to Lady Patrina. Here, I'll show them to you." He opened his bag and then carefully used his fingers to widen the neck of the little pouch to reveal the flowers.

James looked at the slender stems topped by small, round white flowers with an orange tinge in the centre. "That's what we came for?" he asked. "That's why we braved all these dangers and discomforts? I hope the lady Patrina appreciates them."

Carlyon glanced at him, struck by the unenthusiastic tone. He looked back at the flowers and saw for the first time that, although attractive, they were not immediately impressive. "We have the flowers and there's an end of it. Think of the tales we'll be able to tell. The prize itself is not important. It's the gaining of it that matters. We've triumphed, and in doing so we've restored a daughter to her mother and we've rid the world of an evil witch. Now I can return and claim my lady."

"That's so. God grant we have a safe return."

"Amen to that." Carlyon began to fasten up his bag again, and said, "We'll make all speed now. There's nothing to delay us. I doubt me that ought else can cross our path to divert us."

# 20

Buoyed up by the way that things had turned out, Carlyon thought that everything was now running fair for him. After all his dangers and struggles he was returning home, successful and safe. Even the weather was mild, with the scent of spring being carried on the westerly breezes. He and James made good time on their journey south, maintaining their high spirits as all went well, and early one afternoon they saw the buildings of Chertsey in the distance. Spurred on by joyful relief, they were soon clattering across the cobbles of the courtyard which they had left the previous December. When Carlyon reined in Champion, a man came running up to hold the bridle while he dismounted. On the ground, he flexed his muscles and asked after the earl.

"My lord is well, sir. He's gone to visit his cousin in Norfolk, now that my lady Patrina is married."

Carlyon swayed. He clenched his fists, but the roaring in his ears was no less. The man had spoken so casually, as if it were simple news, and he was even now calmly reaching for James's bridle. It seemed to mean nothing to him. It was impossible news, and Carlyon's mind rattled. How long had he been away? How could so much have changed? How could Lady Patrina not have waited for him? She had given her word, just as he had given his.

It was not right. Perhaps she had been forced to marry against her will. Carlyon remembered that her father was a man who was accustomed to getting what he wanted. Perhaps he had found a better match for his daughter? Carlyon did not want to believe that Patrina had betrayed him while he was away, and married another in such a fickle manner.

He drew in a breath and, somewhat squeakily, asked, "This is his only daughter, my lady Patrina, who has married?"

"Yes, indeed, sir. Did you know my lady?"

"Of course I did. I'm an old friend of the family."

Carlyon looked at the servant, who looked back at him respectfully as he would at any stranger. He was surprised that he could not remember seeing the man before. It was almost as if he had returned to the castle as a ghost, or as if many years had passed since he had left. He looked around the yard, seeking signs of change. He was brought back by the sound of James's voice.

"When did my lady marry?"

"Shortly after Candlemas."

Carlyon snapped the man's attention onto him by asking, "Whom did she marry?"

"Sir John le Cerre-nore, a valiant knight, who one time saved my lord the earl's life, so they say, by bravely fighting off a pack of wild boar."

The shock at hearing that his friend had been as good as his word was almost as great as that from the initial news of the marriage. Carlyon had not believed John when he'd said that he would try to win Patrina, and he had trusted Patrina to wait for him. Both of them had betrayed him. He wanted to be alone to deal with it, but first he had to twist normality into his actions and do what was required. He dismissed the man, curtly telling him to lead away the horses and have their bags taken inside. With a brief glance at James, he himself went into the house, where the steward had already been informed of his arrival and was advancing towards him.

"My lord the earl is away from home, sir, but I bid you welcome for him," he announced with a slight bow. "Will you take refreshment now?"

"Thank you, Humfrey," said Carlyon, relieved that at least the steward looked just the same. "But first, I pray you, what news of my lady Patrina and Sir John?"

"They are well, sir, and living in the earl's house near Maidenhead."

"I had not expected to hear of this marriage. I've returned with a prize for my lady."

"Indeed, sir." The steward inclined his head respectfully and said no more.

Carlyon thought that he detected sympathy for him in the man's tone. He guessed that the steward knew of the quest, but felt that it was not his place to comment. Carlyon pressed his lips together and struggled to find a way of asking for more details without appearing too emotionally involved. "I'll warrant the wedding was a grand affair."

"It was a fitting celebration, sir. My lord did all that was proper for my lady, his daughter."

"I had not expected a wedding so soon." Carlyon paused, but the steward said nothing, so he went on, "I shall pay Sir John and his wife a visit."

"I've heard that Sir John is away from home. He has gone to France with the King. They say that a military campaign will begin soon."

Carlyon looked away thoughtfully. He wanted to be alone to come to terms with all these unexpected happenings. Speaking more robustly than he felt, he told the steward to prepare rooms for him and James and said that they would leave on the morrow.

After supper that evening he sat with James for a while. Since their arrival, James had been busy relating his adventures to whoever would listen, and in return he had learned much about what had been happening during their absence. He told all this to Carlyon, who affected indifference.

"Lady Patrina loves another, not me. So it is."

"I can scarce believe it. I was sure she loved you, sire."

"Mayhap she did. But when love takes lodging in a woman's heart, it's often but a passing guest. I should have been here, to press my suit and to make sure no rival took advantage. I was absent and there's an end of it. Even so, I don't regret the search for the flowers, frivolous though the vow now seems. I did my duty. I'm glad for what we achieved and the people we met."

"Perhaps we should have stayed in the north. I'll warrant there would have been more work for us."

Carlyon looked at him stonily. He knew that to have stayed in the north would have been to stay close to Mary, but he also knew that it was too late for that now, and he shook his head. "We can't go back. We've left all that behind. We'll to my father's on the morrow. First I'll away to see where the lady Patrina is living."

Lady Patrina was living in a fortified manor house near Maidenhead. It had been one of her father's properties, and he had given it to his daughter as part of her marriage settlement. She had been pleased at how quickly her husband had begun to treat it as his own; happy to live there until his own inheritance fell due. It made her feel good that she was easily able to do such things for him. Now, on an April morning, Lady Patrina was sitting at a window which overlooked the River Thames. She was looking out on the river as it flowed unheedingly past, bright in the early spring sunshine. The pleasantness of the view was there in her thoughts, but did little to lighten them.

Marriage was not how she had dreamed it would be. John had installed his own chamberlain to run the house and Patrina was allowed to give no orders other than to her own maid. She was beginning to feel that she was simply her husband's chattel, and that she had had more freedom in her father's house. John's behaviour towards her had also changed, although if she was honest, he had given signs of an arrogant, uncaring nature while he was courting her. The influence which she had expected to have over him had proved to be no more substantial than a morning mist. She seemed unable to do anything to restore her dream of being worshipped. He had even told her that he had married her for her dowry.

She could not prevent the thought entering her mind that Sir Carlyon's soul would have been free of such a mundane consideration as a dowry. He would have been aloof to such things. He had had a dream – she could almost call it a vision – that he should do something special for his lady love. She remembered how John had scoffed at Carlyon's claim. Others too had not taken him seriously. He had been a voice crying in the wilderness. But she had believed in him. She wondered now how he had fared in his search, undertaken for her. Her breast was touched by a shiver of regret that she had not persuaded her father to wait a little longer, to see if he would return.

She glanced down at the hand which bore the ring that John had given her on their wedding day. There was nothing else. Now he had abandoned her to go fighting in France and forbidden her to leave the house in his absence. She was conscious of being spied on by those members of the household staff who owed their loyalty to her husband rather than to her. When she moved about the house, the memories of the happy times that she had spent there on visits in her childhood were smothered by an oppressive blackness that shrouded and distorted them. Her husband's presence seemed to have touched everything, even though he was such a recent tenant.

Often it was a relief to sit by her window, as she was now doing, and look out at the life beyond. The occasional boatman on the river, and the cattle on the far bank, were like ladders to an attainable freedom. One day her white knight would come to rescue her. This was a dream with which she played as if she were fingering a necklace of precious stones glittering in the sunlight. She was sure that one day Sir Carlyon would come.

Carlyon was on the riverbank by a bend in the river. He was sitting on a large stone, just out of sight from Patrina's window and unaware that she was there. Thoughtfully he watched as the river flowed by, unheedingly taking the water past her window.

"Will you be calling in to visit the lady Patrina, sire?" asked James at last, diffidently breaking into his master's introspection.

Carlyon jerked his head to look at him, as if the words had been a fishing line catching him. He said nothing at first, while he pulled himself back into the world and out of the depths of his dreams. "I think not, James," he told him reluctantly. "The lady Patrina has chosen Sir John instead of me. I must respect her choice and accept that she's rejected me. She sent me to collect the flowers of the swan, but she waited not for my return. I thought I had been given a duty to perform, a duty that would show the purity and uplifting power of love. I was deluded, unable to distinguish a dream from what was actually real. It was a silly and trivial vow and I've collected and brought the flowers in vain for a love that was no more than a floating bubble which burst while I thought it safe in my hands."

He smiled ruefully at James, who remarked sympathetically that they had had a lot of bad luck in their search for the flowers.

"Mayhap so, but we had a goodly portion of fair fortune too. No – I was unable to win the lady Patrina because I did not carry out my task properly."

"How is that, sir? You have the flowers in your pouch."

"I know not. I'm not sure of anything now. Yes, I have the flowers, but what fortune have they brought me?" Doubt was a cold fog drifting behind Carlyon's eyes and closing down his vision. He was looking out over the river, but taking note of nothing that he saw. Perhaps he could have been more scrupulous in how he had undertaken his search. It would then have been possible to ward off the bad luck that taking the flowers had brought. He was interrupted again by James, who moved restlessly beside him and blew his nose. Carlyon's eyes seemed to snap open and he set his mouth resignedly. "Well," he said. "Here we are and here it must be. Take the horses into town and order lodgings for this night. We'll leave for my father's on the morrow. I'll walk along the riverbank awhile and join you later."

When he was left on his own, he remained seated where he was. It was calming to watch the river, and his intention to walk by Lady Patrina's home was held for a while, as if the rolling waters were holding him in a trance. As he sat, he thought over how he

237

had declared his love for her, and how he had had such high hopes for its success. Now his dreams were scattered like splashes of water on a stone that would soon be dried up in the sun. He pulled in his lips. There was nothing for it – he had to accept that all was lost. Patrina loved John, not him. John had acted with speed and had been successful. As he came to that conclusion, Carlyon lifted his head to look down the river to where it turned to flow past Patrina's home. There seemed to be no hope there.

He reached into his little pouch and took out the flowers of the swan. They were still looking healthy, despite their journey, and cradled in his hands they had a beauty that was mocking him. Patrina would certainly have been pleased with them. Irritated, he shook his head, as if to dismiss such thoughts. She would not be getting the flowers. She would never see them. As she had made her decision, so it must be.

Slowly, he got to his feet. He also made a decision. He would go home to his father's. From there, perhaps he would make arrangements to join the King in France and seek glory on the battlefield. But first, there were the flowers. He looked down on them and gently blew out his breath in a derisive snort of resignation. They were of no further use to him, and he climbed up onto his rock to look down on the river a few feet below him. Almost lovingly, he lifted the flowers momentarily to his face and then stretched out his arms. Seemingly without thought, he let his hands open and the flowers dropped into the water. As they were carried away, his body almost appeared to sway forwards, as if attempting to follow them.

Keeping his eyes on the flowers, he turned to leave. As he moved, his feet slipped on the mossy rock. Unable to regain his balance, he fell, catching his head sharply on the rock. At first he did not know what was happening. It was as if his mind were elsewhere, floating in the air behind the flowers. He could not understand why there was water in his mouth, making him cough; why his clothes were unexpectedly heavy on his body, pressing him down. As his woollen garments filled with water and liquid seeped into his lungs, there was an instinct to struggle, to fight, but then it seemed easier to surrender and let himself go. Gentle peace wrapped around his soul like gossamer-soft petals and he closed his eyes beneath the water.

Soon there was nothing to be seen on the surface of the river but six flowers. As if they were bearing the souls of dead lovers, they were carried round the bend by the current. The river flowed on, impassive and inexorable. Lady Patrina, sitting at her window, saw no flowers. But as she pensively looked over the river, seven swans came into sight and glided serenely past. She watched them, their pure beauty briefly calming her agitated breast.

Out of her sight, she knew nothing of a young woman who was standing on the riverbank where Carlyon had been. She was dressed simply in a grey woollen shift, but her blue eyes and light brown hair fastened in two braids gave her an attractiveness that was enhanced by her slightly crooked nose. She looked out over the river, holding the tip of her thumb between her teeth, as if in thought. Then she bent to pick up a flask of water which had been left on the bank with a small pouch. A beautiful smile shone on her face as she lovingly cradled the flask. It was as if she had been seeking it and knew that she would be able to use it.

Slowly she began to walk downstream, towards where the swans had gone. She did not see the lady who was looking out of a window, and who was thinking nothing of the peasant woman, the simple thatcher's daughter, walking past, so near that she could have called out to her. The lady, locked in her own sadness, thought nothing of it when she saw the woman pick up a swan's feather that had blown onto the riverbank. She did not know of the new quest which was about to begin.

www.ingramcontent.com/pod-product-compliance
Lightning Source LLC
Chambersburg PA
CBHW020653030726
47498CB00002B/488